The patterns on Foundry Edition's covers have been designed to capture the visual heritage of the Mediterranean. This one is inspired by the architecture of Santiago Calatrava's City of Arts and Sciences in Valencia. It was created by Hélène Marchal.

ROSA RIBAS was born in El Prat de Llobregat, just outside Barcelona, in 1963. She has a degree in Hispanic Philology from the University of Barcelona and lived for thirty years minus two months in Frankfurt, where she wrote her PhD, and taught at the Goethe University and the Instituto Cervantes. She now lives and works in Barcelona again and the city plays a big role in her writing. Rosa is widely considered one of the queens of Spanish noir and has achieved great critical and commercial success in Spain with her *Dark Years* trilogy (Siruela) and her *Hernández* trilogy (Tusquets).

CHARLOTTE COOMBE works from Spanish, French and Catalan into English. She was shortlisted for the Queen Sofía Spanish Institute Translation Prize 2023 for her co-translation with Isabel Adey of *December Breeze* by Marvel Moreno. In 2022 she won the Oran Robert Perry Burke Award for her translation of Antonio Díaz Oliva's short story 'Mrs Gonçalves and the Lives of Others', and she was shortlisted for the Valle Inclán Translation Prize 2019 for her translation of *Fish Soup* by Margarita García Robayo.

FAR

ROSA RIBAS

Far

Translation by Charlotte Coombe

FOUNDRY EDITIONS

A Klaus, siempre cerca

1

That night, he had no idea he was walking over a cemetery. A secret cemetery with no gravestones or crosses, and only two dead bodies. There would be three by the time he left.

He kept walking until he felt tarmac beneath his feet. The rustling of dry grass that accompanied his footsteps was replaced by the sound of chirping crickets. His shoulders ached. He stopped and put down the rucksack and duffel bag he was carrying. In the bag he had packed clothes, shoes, and a washbag; in the rucksack, food for the first few days and, beneath the tins and packets, the money.

In this part of the residential development, the buildings were unfinished and there was no light coming from any of the windows, no street lamps to give him away in the darkness of the new moon. He rolled his sore shoulders, stretched his neck and arms. Everything crunched. He took a deep breath, picked up his luggage again, and followed the tarmac road flanked on the right-hand side by a metal fence that enclosed the unfinished buildings. He looked straight ahead, sensing the darkness sealing shut behind him like the zip on a body bag.

The apartment he was looking for was in the boundary zone, in a part of the development where the blocks were finished but half empty. He came to the end of the long fence and turned right. He was greeted by a row of headless lamp posts, metal poles along a ribbon of pavement, interrupted at regular intervals by rectangles of earth where benches should have been. On one of these, a resident had lined up three plastic chairs. He didn't know whether to find this pathetic or frightening.

He made his way up the street, sticking close to the walls. On the opposite side of the road he saw something unexpected: a brightly lit window on the third floor. An insomniac, perhaps, or someone who kept the lights on to chase their fears away like children do. In those initial blocks, few of the apartments were occupied. He was afraid the insomniac might peer out and spot him. But why would they be looking out of the window at three in the morning? At what? Their improvised bench, perhaps.

He took out the keys, carefully, so they didn't jangle against each other. The metallic sound might alert one of the few neighbours, might rouse the insomniac from their incipient slumber. In front of the door he felt a jolt of panic. What if the key didn't work? Thinking about it, he should have left the copies with Luján, who never came out here, and taken the originals himself. But the key slid smoothly into the lock, opened it, and allowed him to enter the hall. Cold, despite the summer. Damp, despite the dry air that parched the fields surrounding the development. He closed the door behind him, as the little sign on the glass requested. He shone the torch at the mailboxes. Lots of numbers but not many names. He took the stairs up to the second floor.

Apartment 2, second floor. A pang of dread, key in hand, at the front door. A pang of relief, too, that the lock put up little resistance.

The trapped air inside lay in wait for him, quiet, foul. Although he needed to be extra cautious, he went into the living room and raised one of the blinds an inch or two. It went up gratefully, with no complaints. In flooded the chirping of the crickets frantically rubbing their hindwings and legs, expelling the stagnant air. He breathed in that new air full of sounds. Exhaustion descended on him with every outbreath.

It had been a long journey since he'd boarded the train in the capital. If his colleagues thought to request CCTV footage, they would see him taking a train in the opposite direction. He had then got off at a station in a town he had nothing to do with and where there were no security cameras. He'd already checked. There was no station manager either. In the event that any of the few passengers remembered him, it would be far away from here. But who would take any notice of a silent middle-aged man on a train? After that, he took a bus which brought him closer to the area. He walked the final stretch along farm tracks. On one side, the devastation of the harvested sunflower fields; on the other, the waiting wheat fields, resigned and yellow. He had only come across one man, on a tractor, who had waved at him. He had left behind an area where the landscape was curved into terraced plots. Crags and rocks that the scrubby bushes clung to with the tenacity of small dogs.

Near the development, past some junipers, he crossed fallow fields, some abandoned more recently, where the plants still respected the old furrows. The only visual reference points he had on that vast plain were a few semi-ruined farmhouses dotted here and there, traces of human life on a deserted planet. He decided to hide out in one of them to let the first few hours of the night pass; inside, it was littered with drinks cans and rubbish. He sat leaning against the wall and let the hours go by. He had to get into the development in the early hours of the morning when everyone would be asleep.

Finally, he had arrived. He set his luggage down on a table and took off his shoes and socks. The dust clung to his clammy feet. According to the mailboxes, both the apartment downstairs and the apartment next door were empty; even so, he tiptoed into the bedroom. He lay down on the bare mattress, which greeted him with a damp belch like a drunkard being woken. His colleague Luján had not been in the apartment for months. He hadn't come during the winter because of the cold. Heating the apartment meant heating the motionless air that enveloped its walls, floors, and ceilings. In the spring, Luján had preferred to spend his nights in the capital. And during that hot, hot summer, the apartment was hardly an enticing option with its swimming pool little more than a rectangular hole dug into the inner courtyard of the building. Luján might show up in the autumn. By which time, he would be long gone. The apartment was a temporary refuge until he found a suitable place to spend the next few weeks, a month, maybe two, enough time for them to accept that there was no sign of him in the capital. Later, he could return, contact someone who could provide him with new documents, and leave for good. But that would be later. For now, all he wanted was to sleep.

In his dreams, he was still walking. The scrubland surrounding the development had become a muddy bog. The mud tugged off his shoes and swallowed them in a soft gulp; then it wrapped around his ankles and a slimy tongue pulled off his socks. He looked down at his feet, surprisingly white and clean. He must keep on walking. He plunged one foot into the mud, took a large stride, sunk the other foot in, and pulled out the first. With every step he struggled to heave his foot out. He looked down again and discovered that it wasn't mud, but cement drying. "You keep hold of it," a voice said in his ear. He tried to run. "You keep hold of it," another voice insisted. Footsteps, hard, dusty feet creeping closer. He woke with a start. He sat up on the mattress, which was soaked in his own sweat. "You keep hold of it," the voice repeated. But there was no one there. It had been nothing more than a musty dream determined to wake him.

The sliver of grey light coming through the crack in the blinds warned him that he might have slipped up. He got up slowly, not wanting to make a sound, and went over to the window.

The apartment block opposite was the final one in the inhabited zone. When the few people who lived there looked out of their windows in the morning, they always saw the same view and knew by heart which blinds went up and at what time. The ones belonging to the empty apartments, always immobile, would have blended in with the walls by now.

He took a pair of binoculars out of his rucksack and returned to the crack in the blinds. One by one, he scoured the windows opposite. No movement anywhere. Not even in the home of the insomniac. Between the shutters already faded by years of sunlight and neglect, the open windows were dark rectangles.

Putting the binoculars down on the floor, he pulled the tape on the blind, which, as it had the night before, obeyed meekly, in silence.

He could not go out until it was dark. He lay back down on the bed.

2

As she did every morning, she slammed the garden gate shut, patted her thighs, and started to run.

First, she zigzagged her way through the area of terraced houses where she lived. Then into the part where the large villas were. Each one was a different colour, so nobody got their houses mixed up. Luxurious two-storey villas, with double garages, terraces, balconies, gabled roofs, and dormers; with extensive gardens, with ponds and flower beds; with loungers in dark wood and cast-iron tables and chairs, covered with custom-made cushions for sitting and drinking beers or lemonade in summer. All built nice and far apart.

She carried on through the streets of apartment blocks. The first phase boasted full occupancy. There were gaps in the following blocks, but only a few. The ratio increased into Phase 2, then went down again in Phase 3, with its most recent buildings barely occupied. Phase 4 was filled with unfinished buildings and surrounded by a metal fence. She would not be running in there. She only went into that part when she had to, on special occasions. Not today.

On normal days she would run through the area where, according to the development's plans, there should be a large park with wide paths, gazebos, pergolas, statues, benches, flower beds, fountains, and even a small lake. The paths had been marked out, a few trees planted, the lake dug out, but the rest still had to be imagined. She ran as far as the statue marking the spot where the other entrance to the park should have been, circled the roundabout at the entrance to the development, then back. At that time of the morning, she usually crossed paths with very few of the 236 inhabitants. "Settlers" was what the locals in town called them; at one time they would have been called "outsiders".

That morning she didn't bump into anyone. Anyone who commuted had already left for work. It was the holidays, so the children didn't need to be taken to the school in the local town, and the shops weren't yet open. What other reason could anyone possibly have to leave their homes? Homes built as part of an urban development programme approved in the year 2000, the documents to which were in the hands of a judge investigating real-estate corruption. The entire development was constructed on a pile of poorly concealed sleaze, a chain of bribery, corruption, intimidation, and complicit silences. No ancient manuscripts, no mythical foundations. If these lands had been the scene of some momentous event, back when battles of conquest and reconquest were being fought all over the area, no one had bothered to record it. It was a bleak place, devoid of stories, where it was impossible to satisfy any yearnings for greatness. Although what degree of greatness could anyone begin to aspire to, living in a place called the Residencial Fernando Pacheco?

Fernandos tend to be smug about the name they've been given. This one tacked on his ten-a-penny surname out of smugness about his project. A premature self-satisfaction that was set in stone when he baptised the development.

She had always found it strange when whole towns were named after one person, the way streets are. Don Benito, Pedro Muñoz, Comodoro Rivadavia, or Perito Moreno. At least that last one got the name of a famous explorer. And had a glacier to show for it.

Here, they had three billboards lined up less than a kilometre from the entrance to the development, still advertising apartments for sale. On the middle one, the developer Fernando Pacheco, in a suit and tie, looked out towards the main road. His eyes were bleached white by the sun, but before that he must have been like one of those images of Christ of the Sacred Heart, whose eyes seemed to follow family members around the dining room. Pacheco's outstretched arms pointed to the billboards on either side. The right-hand one depicted a bird's-eye view mock-up of the development. On the left-hand one, a multitude of smiling people, men golfing, kids splashing around in a swimming pool, a mature couple sipping on cocktails while two couples played padel tennis in the background, young families with children strolling through a forest. How could they be so blinkered, seeing only what was on the billboards and not the reality surrounding them? Not even the implausible forest scene snapped them out of their reverie of social ascent.

Most of the colours had faded in the sun. Blue held out, as always. Clever of Pacheco to choose a suit in that colour.

Residencial Fernando Pacheco. Sí, señor. There they were.

The small town was four kilometres away, the capital seventy. *On your doorstep*, the advertisements proclaimed. *Near and far*. Bullshit. It was just far. But that didn't matter, did it, if they had practically everything they needed right there?

Every amenity was promised to the development's residents. Daily amenities, such as supermarkets, bakeries, hairdressers, bars and restaurants, a nursery, and a school. And then other amenities that justified the use of the word "luxury" in the advertising: gyms, swimming pools, cinema, an event space, sports centre with tennis and padel courts, and the inevitable golf course, the wet dream of the nouveau riche.

The idea was that it would be a city in the countryside, with straight city streets, city lamp posts, city benches. She recalled the time, a couple of years ago, when a new resident moved into the terraced houses and decided she would put some chairs out on the pavement like the women did in rural villages, to sit and enjoy the fresh air. She set out three. One for herself and two for anyone else who might care to join her. All week, she waited for someone, anyone, to stop and have a bit of a chat with her. She experimented with every variant: she sat in the chair on the right, then the left, then the middle. From this trio of different positions, she greeted any passing neighbours with the anxious look of a busker who has run out of songs. She gave up on putting out the chairs when a neighbour asked her if she was having work done on her garden.

No, this was no village.

That was the one thing they were under no illusion about: the development made no attempt to simulate rural life. No wagon wheels on the roundabouts or farming tools adorning the parks. The parents there were never meant to stick their offspring in front of some rusty piece of equipment and tell them all about how their grandparents, or more likely their great-grandparents, had used it for ploughing, reaping, threshing, winnowing... Activities as obscure to the children as they were to the parents, who would have had to lie outright if asked "What's that thing called?" and call a hoe a plough or a scythe a sickle to prevent some old piece of junk from prematurely stripping them of their omniscient-parent status.

On the development, it had taken them a while to realise that the work had definitively ground to a halt, even though they'd been subjected to the cicadas for several weeks since the giant insect-like buzzing of the machines had ceased. They had to finally accept it the day a van pulled up in front of the unfinished mini mart and two workmen removed the little red car the children liked to sit on, making vroom-vroom noises or getting their parents to do it, since they all knew that dropping a coin into the slot had no effect.

Ashamed, or angry, someone tore down nearly all the posters bearing the images of singers who had performed at the party organised by Fernando Pacheco for the development's official opening. Promising young stars from TV castings, or old has-been music legends. Pure fiesta fodder.

Then, given the inhospitable environment, efforts became focused on the interior, on the decor of the apartments and villas.

And on the "dignification" of the settlement. Swept pavements, manicured gardens. Being dressed properly in the street.

"So, no more going out in your dressing gown to buy bread," said Sergio Morales, the chairman of the residents' association, at one of their meetings, in that jocular tone which often masks inconvenient or ridiculous orders.

"And no leggings." Raquel Gómez, orange villa (i.e. Phase 1) took the opportunity to throw this in casually, but it was clear she was addressing Beatriz Puértolas, Calle Sorolla number 7, apartment 3, second floor, who immediately stopped chewing her gum.

At the time, Beatriz Puértolas had been living on the development for less than a year. She had bought one of the apartments in Phase 2; apartments sold at bargain prices after the economic slowdown and crisis. They were even sold to young twixter couples, strategically distributed throughout the apartment blocks to prevent deterioration. Like in the age of industrialisation when destitute people were allowed to live for a few months in newly built dwellings so that, like human dehumidifiers, they would remove the moisture from the mortar using their own body heat, and the carbon dioxide through their breathing. Then they would be kicked out and in came the real tenants. The twixters ran water through the pipes, ventilated the spaces, scrubbed the floors, heated the walls, while the developers waited for better times to come.

"We can't have the place turning completely chavvy," Raquel Gómez added.

Beatriz Puértolas said nothing at the time, but the chewing gum started moving defiantly again.

She felt ashamed when she remembered that episode; she should have come to Beatriz's defence, as the two of them had a budding friendship, but she had said nothing. She pretended to be busy taking the minutes of the meeting. Her first minutes. She had just been unanimously appointed secretary of the association. Flattered, accepted, and therefore a coward.

The next day, Beatriz wrote her an email telling her that she was leaving the association. It was so formal, it was almost as if it was written on stiff card. The "yours sincerely" also put a firm end to their friendship. They had not spoken to each other since.

From then on, leggings became a symbol of class rebellion; dressing gowns were the uniform of the resistance, as were men's tracksuit bottoms. It was a hidden war, its battles fought with glances and insinuations, with offhand comments. But it did not cause a rift. Nearby, very near, there lurked a common enemy that kept them united: the squatters, the worrying, menacing presences in the Phase 4 apartment block. This was the forbidden place for teenagers, a substitute for the dark forest or graveyard that every generation needs.

Adolescence is an evolutionary punishment that can only be overcome by passing certain tests. The kids occasionally made forays into the uninhabited blocks, which looked sinister even in daylight. And the parents, naturally, were already telling the story of the child who was playing in one of the unfinished houses, stepped out onto a balcony with no railing, fell, and, of course, died. They already had their first urban legend. Beware, children, don't go near the forest of concrete pillars. You won't find the big bad wolf lurking behind them, but maybe a bogeyman from Romania who will cart you off in a supermarket trolley full of scrap metal.

They scared the children with tales of accidents or terrible encounters with the illegals; she herself was frightened when she imagined getting lost for hours in the barren fields, not knowing which way to walk to reach any of the small towns, which were scattered around the region as if someone had sneezed on a Ludo board.

After her run she showered, ate breakfast, and sat down at her computer. The assignment wasn't complex. The bad thing about easy tasks was that they made her sleepy. No, worse, it was that they didn't entertain her enough, they didn't fully occupy her mind, and that was dangerous because the unoccupied part set to work on its own, thinking about her situation. And that was far from advisable.

She put on her glasses, logged on to her computer, and forced herself to shut out the world.

Another day of getting through it.

3

He was woken by something squawking as it flew past the blind. He had slept nearly the whole day. It was getting dark. He went into the living room, which was dimly lit by daylight from the adjacent kitchen window. The semi-darkness muffled the cheap ugliness of the sofa, little coloured triangles scattered apathetically over its upholstery like confetti left over from a party. Luján had bought all the requisite items for life with a family, even though he did not have one. A sideboard, a three-piece suite, side tables, four chairs around the fat-legged dining table with a blackened silver fruit bowl that looked like a wedding present he'd been obliged to keep because it was from one of his relatives. Luján had been divorced for several years and only ever mentioned occasional one-night stands. Not because he was interested to hear about them, but because Luján was desperate to tell him. "Single at fifty, mate. You and I are at our peak, we're in the prime of our lives." In the capital, that apartment would have been an absolute bachelor pad. But there? So far from everything? Plus Luján, however much he claimed he was in his prime, was no longer at the age when he could spend a whole weekend between the sheets. They might go at it for a couple of hours, tops, then he and the lucky lady would have to kill the rest of the time twiddling their thumbs in the middle of nowhere.

As he ate, he listened keenly to the sounds of the building. The occasional slamming of doors reminded him there were neighbours. Noises also drifted in from outside. Very few: blinds going up or down, voices, the odd car approaching, people coming back from work in the capital.

Finally it was dark. He waited a few more hours, however, before going out to do a recce of the site to check if it was safe.

He toyed with the idea of having a drink. There was a drinks cabinet: one of those old-fashioned ones with a folding door and a mirrored interior that multiplied the bottles and glasses to infinity. He picked up a bottle of vodka but immediately put it down. Dust clung to that too. He wiped his hands on his trousers. He would not drink. On his first outing he needed to have a clear head. Bumping into someone could be fatal. They might alert the police to the fact that an intruder was living there. Then maybe the others would connect the dots.

But otherwise there was no way in hell it would occur to them to look for him in Luján's apartment. Every time the detective sergeant started talking about it during the lunch break, people would roll their eyes. "Luxury development, guys. It's got the whole shebang, swimming pool, golf course, gym..." he said, thrusting his phone in their faces to show them photos of the project. Later, when everything went downhill, he started hounding colleagues to try and persuade them to pay a sort of hourly rate to use the apartment on a "casual basis". He would show them the keys, convinced the mere sight of them was a tempting prospect. The jangling in his jacket pocket was like the song of some dry-land siren.

Luján tried it with him too. Sometimes they would be talking and Luján would start shaking his keys in his pocket while nodding at him: "Come on, mate, you up for it?" That's why, when the situation became dangerous, when he realised they'd pinned it on him, he remembered that apartment out in the sticks.

While Luján was outside having a smoke, he sneaked the keys out of his colleague's jacket and made a copy. He put them back during another cigarette break, and mid-morning, pretending he had work to do out of the office, he went home, packed his bags and fled. The others would not notice he was gone until the following day.

If Luján had been involved in the racket, it would have been pinned on him; Luján had always been the chump of the group. At what point did the other three decide *he* was the chump? What secret signals had they exchanged to decide who was going to be the one to pay for it? Why was he the odd one out? Actually, it wasn't hard to guess: blood. Shared blood. The others had survived a shoot-out together and had felt the spatter of a dead colleague's blood on their faces. He'd arrived on the scene later. Although his hands were as dirty as those of the other three, he lacked the blood spatter, he thought, as he splashed water on his face at the sink.

From the window, he saw that the lights in the inhabited apartments had all gone out. He could just about make out the dark rectangles, wide open to try and catch the slightest breeze that night. There was only the gentle breathing of the building, the creaking of its empty bowels. He went outside.

Walking through the fields that surrounded the development, he avoided the flat stretch close to the road, where he'd be exposed if anyone approached in a car. In the middle of that open countryside were three large billboards advertising the Residencial Fernando Pacheco development.

Pacheco, who had fled abroad on the run from the law, had offered him refuge in his failed urban development project. "Pacheco, that son of a fucking bitch" was what Luján had started calling him when the bubble burst. Well, thank you, you son of a fucking bitch.

Although he had left in a hurry, it seemed like he had chosen a good place. Other developments like this were either being repopulated or were at such an embryonic stage that they were impossible to live in. Here, on the other hand, he could hide out while everyone forgot about him, while his face was erased from the news, if he ever appeared on the news at all. After that, a new identity, a new life.

He had left behind the noise, the shouting, the music, the scents, the fumes, the air fresheners, the unrelentingly firm, hard ground of the city, the rubbing and knocking of shoulders and elbows. Here, only the sound of the crickets and his footsteps. It smelled of earth, of unfamiliar plants. His feet sometimes trod on solid ground; sometimes on dry weeds; sometimes he stumbled as he tripped over holes, burrows perhaps. Beneath his soles he felt the edges of rocks, angular as if they had just been dug out of a quarry, hidden amongst the grass and earth.

Reaching a high point, in the distance he could see the small town that served the development. If he decided to stay, he would eventually have to go into town to buy some supplies. It was a nondescript little town. Low-rise houses in the centre, a church that overcompensated for having been built on such a flat piece of land by having an inordinately large tower. Two newer neighbourhoods, one at each end of the town, with blocks of apartments and functional buildings for facilities. One cube that might be the school, another the health centre, and a third the sports centre. The whole thing cut cleanly in half by the local main road. Half a kilometre away, its neon lights glowing in the night, a small petrol station.

As he stood up to make his way back to the apartment, a stone dug into his foot. It was triangular and sharpened, like a prehistoric tool.

"Where did you come from?"

These were the first words he'd uttered since arriving. He slipped it into his trouser pocket. It would be his amulet, a stone of invisibility so nobody saw him, so they did not find him. The next day he would discover that the stone was marked with a line in blue felt tip.

It was starting to get light. He needed to get back to his hiding place, fast.

He slept badly, the light sleep of the fugitive, waking at the slightest noise: voices, car engines, motorbikes, barks, birds, doors, blinds, the creaking of the building. Only the constant sound of the cicadas lulled him back to sleep, until he was startled by a noise. Or voices in his dreams. "You keep hold of it," Ibáñez said, handing him the bag of money. Ibáñez's gloved hands. He didn't need to ask him why he was wearing gloves, he knew. You keep hold of it, so we can come in the night and bump you off. We'll have tampered with the evidence beforehand, so don't worry, you can die in peace, nothing will happen to us. There will be no fingerprints.

4

"And I propose that it isn't just some of us who organise it, or lots of us, but all of us..."

"As your mayor, I am..."

She needed to focus. If the minutes of the meeting were incomplete she would be blamed. They all read them looking for themselves, and, like film divas, counting and comparing their own lines of dialogue with other people's. This was why she was taking great care over drafting the notes, trying to satisfy everyone, although she suspected she was doing such a good job of it that no one noticed the effort she was putting in, taking what they read as an accurate depiction of how the meetings had played out.

> Sergio Morales, chair of the residents' association, proposes that they hold a neighbourhood festival. Raquel Gómez, member of the board, proposes that it should be a themed party. Ernesto Royo, treasurer, proposes that...

This time, the minutes would be a lot of work for her. The word "proposes" had been used three times. Synonyms. *Morales presents the proposal.* What a rubbish synonym! *Raquel Gómez adds that...* The young couple in the white villa, who looked more like conjoined twins than a married couple, tossed around ideas and gazed at each other admiringly; the lawyer in the blue villa, Ernesto Royo, made amendments, and so it went on until they arrived at the "Wine and Harvest Festival".

The last person to harvest anything round here, she thought, must have been a Roman or one of those ancient Celtiberians they'd learned about in school, who didn't really exist because they were different peoples: the Belli, the Titii, the Suessetani, the Ilergetes, the Sedetani, and the Ilercavones.

She was definitely off her game today. It must be the pills.

> Wine and harvest festival. Ernesto Royo offers to contact the winery belonging to a relative, to organise a wine tasting.

In the category of community buzzwords, "organise" competed fiercely with "normal" for the crown.

"Well," said Morales, "there'll be loads to do, so as soon as we work out what needs doing, we'll divvy it up between us."

> A Festival Committee is formed, made up of all the members of the residents' association.

Everyone? But I... She didn't say anything because someone was urgently asking for the floor.

> Yolanda Vivancos proposes the idea of turning the festival into a kind of "annual festival" for the development. The chairman requests that this be added to the agenda for the next residents' meeting.

Sergio "don't call me chairman" Morales could barely conceal his jealousy over the fact that he hadn't come up with the idea himself. Every compliment about Yolanda Vivancos's proposal was a stab at his ego. Not with a Venetian stiletto or a Malay pirate's kris, but one of those miniature plastic swords used for skewering pinchos. Yolanda Vivancos lived in one of the terraced houses, not in the large villas like him.

"What a great idea, Yolanda!"

Stab, stab. Another tiny sword. Sergio Morales's body transformed into a hedgehog with lurid-coloured spikes, a psychedelic cartoon porcupine. She needed to focus. No pills for her tonight.

And risk having dreams?

"Finally," said Morales in his most officious tone, "we've received a message from Beatriz Puértolas..."

Hearing the name of the woman who'd almost been a friend, she felt a twinge of remorse.

"... asking us to make a petition to the local council."

"About what?" asked Germán Pueyo, a sixty-year-old semi-retired man with hands as hairy as coconuts. He lived in one of the few inhabited apartments in the penultimate block of the development, just before the fenced-off zone.

"Increasing the frequency of rubbish collection," Morales replied.

Silence. Some of them were probably torn between the reasonable nature of the proposal and the hostility they felt towards the person suggesting it. But what's right is right, whoever it comes from.

"I think she's right," she said, lifting her hands off the laptop keyboard.

She looked at the others. Only Raquel Gómez, orange villa, looked disapproving. Not surprisingly, since it was because of her that Beatriz Puértolas had left the association.

"It's true. If the rubbish isn't collected more frequently, it attracts rodents..." said Germán.

A magic word, "rodents", broke the curse. The proposal was approved and the meeting was adjourned shortly afterwards. She hung around for a few minutes adding some finishing touches to the notes, in which, for the first time, her name would appear as one of the protagonists. She secretly enjoyed this minuscule success; it made her feel more integrated.

It was late, but they stayed a little while longer in Morales's villa. Those who were working the next day had to wake up early to get to the capital, but they lingered. The social life of the development was still a tender little seedling and, like many exotic plants out of their natural habitat, it had to be held up by stakes, string and effort.

"We have to see each other and spend good times together."

So there they were, seeing each other.

In any case, no one wanted to be the first to leave the meeting. Leaving meant turning your back. Dangerous. Jesse James was shot in the back as he was hanging up the HOME SWEET HOME sign. It ended up crooked. In that house, nothing was crooked or untidy or stained, and the dust, omnipresent in the development, barely had time to settle on the surfaces before it was wiped away.

She went to the kitchen counter to pour herself a glass of wine.

"When will you have it ready?"

She swung round, alarmed. Sergio Morales's drooping cheeks pulled his large dark eyes downwards; his nose was flat like a dog's, a basset hound's. The rest of him was tucked into a Nirvana T-shirt and ironed jeans. He looked like a posh boy from Madrid, but he was a forty-something man from Santander who was an embarrassment to his teenage kids.

"What?"

"The minutes."

"Tomorrow."

"Good, good."

She seized her chance. "Hey, about organising the party... I'm really busy at the moment and I don't know if I can commit to taking on a lot of work and—"

Morales gave her a slightly hurt look. "Sure, whatever. Although I thought in your situation you might welcome the distraction."

Urge to throw wine over him, punch him in the face, run away. Need to fit in with these people.

"I'm not saying I don't want to be involved, I just don't have a lot of time available... but you can count on me."

"Of course, of course. Sorry, I didn't mean to put pressure on you. I know it's tough."

She would have thrown wine over him, punched him in the face, run away. And yet she said: "Thanks for understanding."

That certainly pleased Morales, who even gave her a couple of fatherly pats on the arm. "Come on, let's go and join the others."

A toast to celebrate the fact they were going to have a celebration.

She left at the same time as Yolanda Vivancos and the young couple. If the devious assassin of Jesse James had been lying in wait to murder anyone from behind, he would have chosen Yolanda Vivancos, who had even gone to the hairdresser's before the meeting. Her dark fringe had gone up several centimetres since the last time she'd seen her. They'd had a salon on the development for two years now. The hairdresser was neither nice nor good at her job, but it was their moral duty to get their hair done there. They kept her in business in spite of the occasional dodgy haircut, the hair pulling, the scalding hairdryer.

She and Yolanda Vivancos both lived in the terraced houses. The young couple insisted on walking the women home, even though they lived in one of the large villas in the opposite direction. The thirty-somethings, both designers (one more technical, the other more artistic), said it was because they didn't want to cut the conversation short; they wouldn't have admitted that it was to protect the women so they would not have to walk that short distance alone, in case there was danger lurking. "Danger" was a forbidden word. "Danger" was a malevolent yet obedient beast that would come if called. "Danger" also referred to the squatters in the uninhabited zone. Nobody knew who they were, or how many there were, but they were an ever-present danger. Because the same fence that hadn't stopped them from getting in hadn't stopped them from leaving either.

They walked along streets lit up like landing strips. Yolanda Vivancos was the first to be dropped off, in the terraced house where she lived with her husband and two teenagers. Then, when they arrived at her door, the conversation stopped. They were no longer interested in the topic; their only concern was her opening the gate to her front garden. They walked off as soon as she turned on the light in the entrance hall.

She went straight to the bathroom cabinet on the first floor. The pharmacy would never have done such a roaring trade in pills before the "settlers" arrived. She wondered whether the doctor who attended the town health centre twice a week had received instructions, or whether she was happy to give them the anti-anxiety medication and sleeping pills because she felt sorry for them. On the other hand, they weren't much trouble. There were hardly any pensioners living on the development, only a few couples had brought their elderly parents with them. Lots of people were convinced the clean air had strengthened their immune systems and was the reason they never fell ill. She thought it was because the microbes from the capital perished before they could reach them. They exploded as soon as they were exposed to this vast horizon, as infinite as outer space.

Two months ago, someone had broken into the health centre and stolen medicines and equipment. Around the development, they said it was one of the "illegals". She believed it was the work of someone local. There wasn't much in the way of fun for the few young people who lived in the town. Unemployment had brought them back there to work in the fields with their parents, when they thought they had left all that behind. The children of rural people do not crave a return to nature. This idealistic notion is the reserve of urban grandchildren.

The issue of the illegals was not discussed with the people who lived in town, out of a mixture of arrogance and fear; the inhabitants of a so-called luxury residential development which had water, rubbish collection, and postal services, thanks to the benevolence of the locals, could not possibly show any chink in their armour. The problem of the illegals was kept hush-hush, just as the owner of a castle never lets on to the masses the extent to which he is plagued by woodworm and leaks.

So they kept their suspicion to themselves. The council put bars on the doors and windows of the health centre and brought in a company from the capital to patch up several holes in the fence that enclosed the squatters' zone: it was not clear whether this was to prevent the existing squatters from leaving, or to prevent new ones from entering. And the doctor went on prescribing pills.

"Only take these in a crisis, and don't mix them with alcohol."

"Of course."

Define a crisis, dear doctor. Besides, she slept much better if she washed them down with a Campari with ice and a slice of orange. A red magic potion. If she drank whisky she'd wake up with a headache and, on her morning jog before starting work, she would feel as if the sun was burning her retinas. Campari and little pills. Dreams of red convertibles cruising across the scorched plain, her wearing a white dress with red polka dots and a red scarf tucked into her hair, the loose strands of her bun whipping her cheeks. Red sunglasses; bushes like corals. She glides along the seabed. It is red. She doesn't care, as long as it's not blue. She dreams of a red sea. But it isn't the Red Sea; not even Moses managed to dye it with his magic wand. Only Campari can do that.

She turned off the lights in her bedroom on the first floor, went out onto the balcony, and sat there in the dark. There, on that desolate treeless plain, it would not be the Santa Campaña that roamed through the night but the funeral procession of Joanna the Mad following the rotten coffin of Philip the Fair, accompanied by the crickets or cicadas, *Ky-rie-ky-rie-ky-rie*. Cicadas, or crickets? One day she would be able to tell them apart. She drowned out the sound by making the ice cubes clink in her glass.

Hers was one of the final houses on the development. At that time of night, her balcony looked out over absolute nothingness.

5

On his next evening walk, he followed the fence around the final part of the development; on the other side there were only incomplete buildings and overgrown piles of construction materials, but in one street he could make out a yellowish glow, as if someone had turned on a dim bulb, like in a post-war boarding house, in one of the unfinished apartments. He spotted several holes in the fence. That's where people were getting in.

In the early hours of the morning he approached the roundabout at the entrance, on the opposite side of the development. If any of the residents were driving home at that hour, he would see their headlights in plenty of time to hide behind the enormous stone letters, spelled out over two lines, on top of a cobbled mound:

RESIDENCIAL

FERNANDO PACHECO

About a hundred metres to the right was the silhouette of a statue on a pedestal. A life-size figure of a standing man. It represented an old farmer with wide trousers, espadrilles, waistcoat, and a shirt with the sleeves rolled up, gazing into the distance, surveying the clouds, which never arrive when invoked by farmers but appear like a herd of buffaloes at harvest time. This was Fernando Pacheco's grandfather, the man who, according to the developer in his hour of glory – when he talked like a winner – had taught him everything he knew. Now the statue of the grandfather contemplated his grandson's failure every day from atop his pedestal.

He sat leaning against the long handle of the stone axe, his back to the non-existent avenue marked by a strip of pavement, and lit a cigarette. At what point would his absence become a disappearance? He had left behind a rented apartment, his belongings, a fridge full of food, his uniform hanging up among the rest of his clothes, his record collection... He'd also left his phone behind: "I'm not an idiot, guys." He regretted not having picked up the battery-powered transistor, an old Sony radio with a broken antenna that he used in the mornings. Perhaps it was for the best.

Finishing his cigarette, he looked up at the statue, but the clouds had covered the still-faint line of the crescent moon and he could barely make it out against the dark background. There was a smell of dampness in the air and the crickets seemed to have gone into overdrive.

Just before sunrise, he returned to the apartment to sleep.

They came back in his dreams. First their feet scurrying in the shadowy recesses of the building. They were looking for him. Luján's keys jangling in other people's hands. Medina opened the door. Ibáñez was holding the bag with the money: "Here. You keep hold of it." Gómez, behind, as always, gun in hand. Ibáñez's gloved hands lifted him up, to take him to a city whose silhouette curved over the horizon as if moving across a dwarf planet, but he resisted, escaping again and again. Medina and Gómez caught him every time.

Cramp in his leg. He awoke with his calf muscles rock hard, his feet burning; he felt the earth sticking to his soles. It was that apartment. He had to get out of there.

6

She woke suffocating. No breeze came through the limp balcony curtains. There was no air. She had to breathe in and out several times to get her brain used to the hot, dry stuff coming in through her nose. She got out of bed as soon as her heartbeat had slowed a little.

When they had moved to the development, she and her husband had taken some walks around the area. They lived out in the sticks, didn't they? One day they walked for several hours without meeting another human being, crossing fields that possibly had owners, given the stone walls between them and the huts for tools and implements. They approached one and found that it was falling down. Inside were empty food wrappers and rusty cans. When they came out of the hut, the sky seemed lower.

"Get me out of here. Let's go home," she said, her voice barely audible.

"You'll have to get up then," he replied.

She hadn't realised her knees had given way. He had to hold her by the arm until the vertigo subsided. After that she walked behind him, her eyes trained on his feet. She could not look up without getting dizzy again, because of the lack of any landmarks. At last they came to a road, and some trees appeared. Then at some point in that blue eternity they glimpsed the development.

Whoever decided that blue was a cold colour had never seen it burn in the summer sky, did not know what it was like to swelter in perennial blue, the eternal days of incandescent fields. They lived under a layer of cling film. They were trapped.

She went down to the kitchen and gulped down two glasses of water.

The previous night she had drunk two Camparis with her pills, and had slept in too late. It was not going to be a good day. The ones that started in a mess never were.

From the kitchen window she could see a totally clear, cloudless sky. The image was identical to that of the previous day. The same bare hills in the background, the same row of saplings along the pavement behind the terraced house. Eleven poplars. Why had they planted eleven? A dozen, a dozen trees, that's what she imagined they'd planned. What kind of architect or town planner decides to plant eleven trees? She ran through it mentally, trying to locate this number in some story or other: the Horsemen of the Apocalypse, sins, muses, magnificent gunslingers, commandments, signs of the zodiac. Nothing was ever counted in elevens. It seemed like the eleventh poplar knew it; it knew full well it was superfluous, inadequate, and so it did not grow as straight as the others.

No, today wasn't going to be a good day.

That's why she never turned on the television, or the radio, which was more dangerous because of the evocative power of music. But despite taking these precautions, the memories came back. Treacherously, like a dirty football player slide-tackling their opponent and bringing them to their knees on the pitch.

Even the expression "dirty player" was a reminder of him. It had worked its way into the dictionary of their shared language as a couple. Throw the dictionary on the bonfire! But that didn't work; there was always one page that wouldn't completely burn.

The dirty player had kicked her in the chest and left her lying there, on that endless pitch. On top of that, she was given a penalty: debts and a mortgage. Ref! Are you blind? Banned for... how many seasons? Fucking dirty player! She couldn't erase it. She had just gone over it again in ink. Well, fine, she would keep it and use it every time she thought about him.

It was past 10 a.m. and already too hot to go running, but she forced herself to go for a walk. She had to get out of the house. Every day, morning and evening. She had to talk to the neighbours, she had to go to the hairdresser's, she had to go to the bar, from time to time she had to go into town shopping, "to spend money, which is a way of supporting the local economy, but oh no, don't call me chairman."

Her house was one of twelve – not eleven – terraced houses in a staggered arrangement, in six rows of two. They were identical little houses, each with a ground floor and upper floor, a garage at the front, and a garden protected by high walls and metal fencing at the back. Hers was in the furthest row, looking outward from the development; it was the closest to the surrounding fields. The lookout in case the Tatars invaded. For more than half a year her house had been the only guard post. The house next door was empty.

The neighbours, a young couple, had left three months after her husband left her. They had also planned to do it like him, to sneak off without saying goodbye. Perhaps it was contagious.

They were found out several weeks before; they were not as devious as her ex-husband, but then again, it's easier for one person to run off and leave the other stranded. It's always easier to empty a few drawers when the other person trusts you completely and would never think to check anything. All you have to do is go to the capital one day and not come back. She was paralysed. Not so much by what had happened, but by how. She was not able to overcome the heartbreak, the pain of accepting that he could leave her in that way. She had gone through break-ups before, but she had never been dumped in a nightmarish version of the joke about the man who popped out to get cigarettes. All alone, with a message that concluded with the words *This isn't the life I want. I'm leaving.*

The neighbours, on the other hand, got caught. The price they paid for leaving the development was the disdain of the others and ostracism. They were declared deserters, undeserving of the meat they'd eaten at barbecues, the clinking of wine glasses when they'd made a toast, the applause they'd received at neighbourhood ping-pong tournaments.

She walked past the Moroccans' bar. She would have loved to stop for a coffee, but didn't want to because she hadn't done anything productive yet. She told herself again that she was going for a walk to clear her head before she started work. She quickened her pace to make it feel more like exercise.

When she reached a small square, she spotted the UPS-brown uniform of the gardener, a skinny, dark-necked fifty-year-old man with bow legs who lived in Phase 2. The community had hired him to take care of everything to do with the plant world on the development. He lived in an apartment he and his wife had bought by trading in their place in the capital as part payment. For them, there was no going back.

She would have liked to avoid him, but he'd already seen her and was raising his hand in a disproportionately large wave, given the short distance that separated them.

"It almost rained yesterday," he boomed, pointing despondently to the hose he was about to be obliged to use.

"And in the end, nothing, not a drop," she heard herself reply, as she did every time they had this exact conversation.

"First things first," he went on, "let's tidy this up a bit here."

A tuft of small grasses bowed their heads, begging for mercy. Those sentenced to death are usually given a final supper, but the gardener, with the indifference of a servant obeying orders, cut them down before watering them, so the invaders would not absorb a single millilitre of the community's water.

"How's work?" he asked, as he chucked the little plants into the bucket for composting.

"Good." She thought she'd better add something else. "It's so quiet here, I get so much work done. I'm making good progress."

She'd also given this reply in previous conversations. All that mattered was that she sounded convincing, that people knew she was all right, and the gardener was a good spokesperson for that. Because she wasn't taken in by this humble-peasant act; she knew he was Sergio Morales's confidant. He was the community's seismograph. She was sure it was the gardener who'd betrayed her neighbours' surreptitious movements as they prepared to escape. He would spy on them when he mowed their lawn or brought round fertiliser for the apple tree they'd planted in the garden, and report back to the "chairman".

One evening, the couple had turned up for a barbecue at Sergio Morales's house.

"So, you're up and leaving without telling anyone?" he said as soon as they arrived.

The man stammered; the woman turned red and clutched her bowl of mango salad. They left the get-together under the disapproving gaze of the other guests. No one spoke to them again. And one day a removal van turned up, and they left.

The gardener was head down, inspecting the gaps between the paving slabs for weeds.

"Anyway, I must be getting on," she said.

"Of course, back to work. But you'll be giving us a hand at the party, won't you?"

"Two, actually," she replied, trying not to let him detect the rage that was creeping up her throat. What were they saying about her around the development?

They smiled at each other as if in a staring match. First to look away loses. In the end it was a tie, because, before the situation became too absurd, the gardener asked her, "When do you want me to come round and cut the hedge? It's looking like it could do with a trim."

When he wasn't busy pulling up weeds, the gardener would patrol the streets inspecting the gardens and hedges. Snooping.

"Whenever works for you." She walked a little way off, repressing the urge to run her hand through her own dishevelled hair.

"I'll leave a note in your letter box."

She continued her walk.

At the roundabout, at the foot of one of the letters spelling out the name of the development, she noticed a cigarette butt. She nudged it with her foot so it was more visible, right in front of the *P* for Pacheco. The gardener would be furious.

The gardener was a Pacheco-ist. A member of a church that had lost nearly its entire congregation. As a professing member of a dying faith, it was up to him to pray, preach, officiate, and persecute heretics, all at the same time.

The Pacheco-ists lived in hope that the developer would return one day to finish what he started. He will return, the good king; like Arthur, or Sebastian I, or Frederick Barbarossa, or Elvis himself; he is not dead, but only sleeping. One day the king will rise and the horizon will once again be crowded with cranes, and the trucks, bulldozers, drills, and construction workers will return to finish the buildings, tarmac the roads, put in benches, street lamps, slides, swings, and rubbish bins. An army of gardeners will be at his command, digging and planting flowers and shrubs in the beds and borders, the roundabouts, the gardens, the large park. And in the end Don Fernando Pacheco will come in person to thank the gardener for taking care of everything in his absence.

Sometimes she felt a little sorry for the blinkered idealism of this poor Pacheco-ist. Pacheco, facing prosecution, had fled the country leaving behind his houses, a yacht, and a fleet of luxury cars composed solely of Mercedes, because that was his mother's name. He also left behind an office building full of suddenly unemployed staff, and this unfinished development.

Sorry, buddies, he won't be coming back. Just like her ex-husband hadn't come crawling back to her, filled with regret.

No, Don Fernando wasn't coming back. King Arthur would be more likely to return before he did.

7

He slept until sunset. Another day spent marinating in his own sweat and the smell of dust. He had not raised the blind again. He washed himself sitting on the floor of the shower so the water made no sound. He waited for a car to go past in the street before flushing the toilet. He took his time eating. He had provisions for two weeks; after that, he would go to a supermarket in town.

The images in his nightmares were still very vivid. He did not see them as premonitions but rather started to believe he was warning himself that the place was not as safe as he'd thought. Luján might decide to turn up there. Or someone might finally take him up on his offer, if only because they'd been hypnotised by the jangling keys. Or it might be precisely Luján's insistence on getting someone to take that apartment "in the arse end of nowhere" that would give Ibáñez and the others the idea, as it had him. They would be frantically trying to find him. Without the money, without someone to blame, the internal affairs people would eventually turn their attention to them. He needed to leave that apartment and find a new hideout. That night he would scope out the area where the uninhabited apartment blocks were.

In the early hours of the morning he left the apartment and made his way downstairs in the dark. Behind a door on the first floor, he could hear voices and the sound of a television. He walked quickly past in case whoever was on the other side sensed his presence with the movement of the air. The television cast a surreal light out onto the deserted street, as if a storm was brewing. He looked at the group of three chairs. They were cheap patio chairs, in white monobloc plastic. They were attached to each other with a chain woven through the backrests. If someone wanted to steal one they'd have to take all three, like in some kind of prison escape comedy.

The uninhabited apartment blocks were one street away. Again, he took the precaution of walking close to the walls. He then followed the fence, shining his torch on it until he located a hole. He wrestled with the pliers he'd taken, until it was wide enough for him to slip through.

He turned off the torch and walked towards the yellowish light he'd seen the night before. It was coming from one of the blocks that were almost finished. The light flickered like gas lamps. He approached slowly, feeling out the ground with his feet. The driveway was in a bad state.

The pavements had withstood the neglect slightly better, but several times he kicked or stepped on loose objects. Rubbish.

As he drew closer he heard voices. He stood still, trying to make them out. Four, maybe five men. Two spoke with a foreign accent. Romanian. He carried on. As he reached what looked like a square, he heard a harsh, dry sound. He stopped. The sound again. It was like someone scraping a giant match. He turned on the torch and saw the blinking eyes of a rabbit staring at him from a cage made out of boxes and wires. The light woke the chickens in a makeshift henhouse. He turned it off and moved away before the animals could alert their owners.

A couple of streets away, more traces of human presence: three chairs placed in front of the entrance to an apartment block. These were made of wood rather than plastic, but they were also close together, as if this parallel universe somehow replicated the one on the other side of the fence. All around, cigarette butts.

He decided to look in a more inhospitable area, where it was less likely there would be people in the apartments. About four or five streets away, the facades were bare, the windows had no glass in them. The ground floors were also boarded up, but many blocks did not even have doors, only bars and hard plastic mesh covering the ground-floor windows. He looked all around the area, finding nothing to indicate that there were other people living there. Maybe he could find a safe place to hide.

He approached one of the doors and tugged on the metal structure. It creaked, his hand got covered in rust and dirt, but it did not open. He made his way along the street. More rough brick walls interspersed with metal bars. He felt the surfaces for any sign of weakness, but the buildings had become fortresses.

When he came to the end of the street, he sat down for a smoke on a step at the entrance to one of the buildings. He sat back against the metal grille. He imagined a pair of hands silently slipping through the bars behind him and tightening around his neck, and although it seemed ridiculous, he stood up.

He continued the inspection with his cigarette between his lips and his hands in his trouser pockets. The body would be in charge of calming the mind. Another block. More boarded-up ground floors, more metal bars, but this time with no planks of wood behind them.

In one of the blocks, the entrance to the underground car park was precariously sealed off with sheet metal, which he easily removed. Total darkness. He switched on his torch to go down the ramp. It smelled musty, a good omen which was confirmed when a rhythmic sound guided him between the pillars of the parking spaces and to some stopcocks and a rusty tap letting out a drop of water every few seconds. The building had a water supply.

As he turned the tap, a jet of water cascaded down into the hole bored into the concrete floor by the droplets, causing it to overflow and soaking his shoes. He spun round, splashing and kicking about in the puddle. The light from his torch cast a deformed, hatless Gene Kelly onto the walls of the car park.

He had a new hideout.

Outside, he went to the entrance gate of the block and struggled fiercely with the grille until he broke the lock. It opened with such a high-pitched screech that even the crickets fell silent. He hurried into the lobby and from there watched for any reaction. Nothing. At some point the crickets accepted that the sound didn't herald the coming of their god and returned to their routine prayers. Like all the buildings, this one had five floors, with four apartments on each floor. The lift shaft was sealed off with planks. At the back, the stairs led upwards. The banisters had no handrail to make the metal structure more user-friendly, but it was enough to prevent him getting vertigo.

On the first floor, signs of a ferocious looting. Wires and pipes had been ripped out, tracing hollow geometric patterns on the walls. Even the window frames were gone.

The second floor looked similar, perhaps more ravaged, as if the looters had been more intense because they were running out of time.

On this floor, however, they had not only taken everything they could find but had also left something behind: a play kitchen. It was propped up against a partition wall, giving the place the dimensions of a Parisian apartment. The beam of his torch illuminated the tiny hobs, the colourfully painted cupboard doors, the plastic sink, the water tank connected by a small, yellowed pipe. He touched the surface to make sure it was covered in a thick layer of dust, to check that when he burst in he hadn't scared away a child who'd been playing there. His imagination was unable to make up a story, any story, to explain why this object was there.

He went up one more floor.

On the third floor the party had ended abruptly. Although all the windows were missing, the wiring had only been ripped out in one of the apartments. In the others, the walls were intact.

He decided he would stay in the apartment furthest from the stairs. To prevent anyone from knowing he was there, he chose to sleep in a room that overlooked the inner courtyard. There was enough wood lying around to cover the window.

Going down to the second floor, he picked up the play kitchen, went back upstairs, and left it propped up by the front door. This is where I'll stay, he thought.

8

Still drowsy, she took out her mouth guard and rotated her jaw several times, ruminant-like, to loosen it up. Her finger joints ached slightly; she'd been sleeping with her fists clenched again. She went to the window. There were a few clouds scattered across the sky. She did not try to see shapes in them; they were just clouds. Far off in the distance, the hills looked like cardboard cut-outs.

The previous night she'd delivered the finished project to the company. Ahead of deadline. Swot. Arse-licker. Teacher's pet. Yeah, so what? She had another project lined up, but she always needed a little bit of downtime before she moved on to the next thing.

She went for a run, did some shopping in town, and had a coffee at the bar on the development. "You must support, you must support, but don't call me chairman." After lunch she spent close to an hour deliberating over which series to watch. Everyone who lived there subscribed to at least two streaming platforms. At the meetings they usually talked about what they were watching and shared a curious yearning for the cinemas in the capital, which they'd not even visited that much because the cinemas they longed for were the ones from their childhood.

The sound of an approaching engine made her look away from the TV screen. The vehicle stopped in front of her garden. She heard tools. The gardener arriving to tidy up, as promised. If a friend is the person who finds you dead in bed after not hearing from you for three days, did this meddling busybody count as her friend? And if she said this to the doctor, would she be prescribed antidepressants there and then, or get sent to a psychologist first?

She went out to say hello. She offered him coffee and made herself a cup as well. She apologised for not giving him a hand.

"Don't worry, I'll take care of it. Work comes first."

That insinuation again? She was about to tell him how she'd already been assigned a task for organising the party. Yolanda Vivancos, who was in charge, had asked her to organise a tombola: "It's to do with numbers and probabilities, so I thought you'd enjoy it." She'd agreed to do it. She would have done it anyway, even if it had nothing to do with numbers and probabilities.

She didn't say anything because she assumed the gardener already knew. She watched his movements from behind the blind. At one point, the man laid his secateurs on the ground, attached the hose to her outdoor tap, and started watering the fugitives' garden next door. He had a gardener's soul and simply could not let those plants, abandoned to their fate, wither and die: the young apple tree, roses, and daisies obligatory in every garden.

All those gardens, separated by walls and fences in the middle of an endless expanse of earth and scrubland, as absurd as cruise ship swimming pools in the middle of the ocean. They were an affront to nature and were consequently punished by the sun, which desiccated anything they planted. The clouds, even those that arrived swollen with water like pregnant elephants, usually rolled on by. But when they dropped their load, they unleashed it with fury; with hatred, you could say.

In towns, the houses turn their backs on the weather; they get the better of the wind with streets that twist and turn like the winding roads that disorientate Chinese dragons; they repel the sun with white walls; the roofs, like tortoise shells, are indifferent to the rain. On the development, the little houses were lined up like the infantry soldiers of a ruthless king. They were the poor sods who ran around screaming until cannon fire blew them sky-high or they were beheaded by sword-wielding horsemen. She remembered a scene from a film she'd watched a few years earlier with her mother, in the hospital she would never leave. Napoleonic soldiers in their flamboyant uniforms, with their Hollywood-white trousers and waistcoats, high boots, epaulettes, plumes. Endless buttons! They marched, bayonets at the ready, then fell down dead and got covered in mud. From the hospital bed, her mother had turned and given her a dismayed look. "What a waste of uniforms! They could have just sent them out in civvies, seeing how long they lasted on the front line."

But it's the front line the enemy sees.

Whenever a storm came, the residents of the development cowered in their beds, feeling how small and helpless they were, out there in the middle of nowhere. The storm could sweep them away like a stream of water carries off a fly wandering gormlessly around a sink. When it thundered, the walls shook, and parents pretended to be brave for their frightened children. Those like her, who had nobody to pretend for, gave in to the fear.

They lived in the countryside and were terrified of it. That is why one of the residents' main worries was that their cars might break down. They subjected them to constant check-ups, as if their vehicles were hypochondriacs. Massive SUVs which had languished in the city, picking up the kids from school. Formerly objects of hatred or mockery because they were so bulky, so fat-arsed, these cars experienced a sort of rebirth on the development. Nothing grandiose though. The intimidating size of their boots might suggest the transportation of freshly slaughtered cattle. Instead they were filled with purchases made with the faux cordiality townies use when dealing with country folk, and that in turn is met with the genuine cordiality that large figures on the cash register prompt in every shopkeeper, rural or urban.

Some people still clung to the belief that the supermarket would open on the development some day. It was built, but there were still so few residents... In the meantime, for essentials, they had the convenience store opened by a Pakistani guy on the ground floor where, according to the development brochure, there was supposed to be some kind of boutique. The man's name was Ahmed; his wife, Laila. In a city, they would be nameless. Sometimes people might ask their name and drop it into conversation with their friends: "I'm going to Ali's" or "I bought it from Mohamed." This made them feel like better people.

Just as the SUVs had found their purpose again here, the Pakistanis had reclaimed their names. As had the Moroccans who ran the bar, Dounia and Khalid.

The Moroccans who ran the bar lived in the local town and rented the premises once it became abundantly clear there would be no organic-clothing boutique or Japanese restaurant on the development. The villa residents turned their noses up at the bar, but ended up going there because it was the only place where they could drink coffee that wasn't out of the magnificent, shiny machines that stood pride of place in all their kitchens, competing with the latest generation of blenders.

The villa residents had the feeling the Moroccans were laughing at them behind their backs. *We can leave whenever we want. You can't.* They also felt like this was hidden behind kindness and smiles, and the use of the word "friend".

"I'll have a cortado, please."

"Coming right up, my friend."

"How much is that?"

"One fifty, my friend."

Then they went back to houses that were gradually taking ownership of them; houses where there was nothing to do, because a villa, however big it may be, isn't a cathedral or an airport; houses inhabited by mediocre aspirations, dreams so short-lived, so low-flying, that they didn't deserve to be called dreams. Houses used to kill people by poisoning them with lead in the plumbing, suffocating them with smoke from a clogged chimney, or by simply falling down. Now they bored them to death.

Doorbell.

The gardener, welcome for once. She went out into the garden.

"What do you reckon?"

The hedge was a perfect straight line; the gardener had swept away any remaining twigs and leaves, along with her gloomy thoughts.

She gave him a generous tip. It was also important for the gardener to be happy with her, to tell the others she was a good resident, that she was tidy and polite, that she was one of them.

9

Crouching, he shivered as the final trickle of cold water ran over his chest, onto his right thigh and down his knee onto the shower tray. It was the last time he would be able to shower. He would miss it.

He took sheets, blankets, and towels from Luján's apartment to his new home. He also took two buckets for carrying water, a few kitchen utensils, and a broom. On a whim, he almost took the silver fruit bowl from the dining room as well. But if Luján showed up there, he would immediately notice it was missing. He doubted that he kept a strict inventory of everything else; it looked like old stuff he'd brought from his home in the capital.

Covering a hammer with a cloth first to cushion the blows, he nailed pieces of wood across the window that overlooked the inner courtyard. When he'd finished, he carefully swept it all up and hurled it off the balcony with childish glee. Then he made a bed in a corner using the sheets and blankets.

No nightmares that night, but he did have the sensation of not being alone. He couldn't make out the specific sounds of a presence, nor did he hear footsteps, or scratching, or breathing. But at the same time it was as if he could sense all of those things. In the morning he woke up disorientated and his memory, which it hadn't done in Luján's apartment, ran through his mental Rolodex of all the rooms he'd slept in throughout his life: his own bed or other people's beds, his various homes, as well as boarding houses and hotels, even a tent during a school trip. As if searching for something to cling to before he became aware of where he was, the last image his mind dredged up was his childhood bedroom in his family's apartment.

The discomfort that had plagued him during the night was most likely due to his new surroundings. All the same, he inspected the floor for footprints. Near the jagged skirting board, a trail of tiny paw prints in the dust. He checked his stash of food. He was willing to share his space with a rat, but he wouldn't share his food. Perfectly wrapped, it was untouched.

Using a piece of paper, he wiped away the prints without removing the dust. When he woke up the next day, they were there again. He removed them again. This childish game relieved his apprehension about a hostile presence and turned the rat, whom he declared a friend, into the guardian of his sleep, keeping watch up and down the skirting board.

*

Forty-seven. "Stop making so much noise!" The sounds the body makes when there are no others to drown it out. Every gasp, every inhalation, the tension and undulation of the muscle fibres as they contract and relax during stretches, the creaking of the joints. "Stop making so much noise!" Forty-eight. Forty-nine. Fifty, pause. Then another set. Every day. Discipline. Workout routines designed so prisoners could do them even in their cells. Discipline and routine for the interminable hours in prison. Discipline. Every day an exercise routine at the same time. And breathing as hard as needed because it wasn't a noise. It's only a noise if someone hears it.

He enjoyed the solitude, even if it wasn't as absolute as he would have liked. In addition to the people he'd heard on the first night, he'd seen clothes hung out on a rooftop, and occasionally the smell of food reached him. But so far he had managed to avoid any encounters.

He ventured out in daylight, always keeping to the overgrown areas and carrying the stone with the blue markings in his trouser pocket. With every walk he took he felt more in control of his space and time. His senses were getting sharper, revealing new nuances of the landscape that he hadn't noticed before. He could distinguish plants and birds. He didn't know their names, but he didn't need to. He discovered the arid beauty of a hill covered with dry grass, like a head with a comb-over; the whimsical formations of the rocks that seemed to move every day; the hole in the ground that the ants circled around like tourists visiting the

Grand Canyon. Occasionally he'd let out an exclamation. His voice sounded flat because the air was so clear that it seemed incapable of holding it, letting it fall to the ground, where it was swallowed up by the earth and the dry bushes. He started talking out loud to himself. It only took a few days before he lost all sense of shame.

At home he was greeted by the little play kitchen, a reminder that other people had also been there for whatever reason. But whoever it was, they had left the place a long time ago.

That night, arriving back at his refuge, he checked – this had already become a ritual – that the wood still covered the window properly, and only then did he turn on his torch. He took one of the cloths he'd brought from the apartment and cleaned the little kitchen thoroughly, opening all the doors and rubbing the tiny handles with determination until they were shiny. This determination made sense when he remembered that, as a boy, he had broken a similar toy belonging to his sister. An act of reparation only he would know about.

It was too hot to fall asleep, so he sat down behind the orange plastic netting that covered the balcony, with his back against the door frame. At some point he was overcome by exhaustion and fell asleep. He was woken by a distant cracking sound. He looked down, expecting to see someone moving along the street. But the noise was coming from the sky; a storm was approaching.

10

The monotony of her days was beginning to strain her eyes and numb her mind. Going for a run, working, walking, having banal conversations with neighbours, a call from friends in the capital who promised to visit her one of those days but in reality were trying to coax her out of the hole she had fallen into, or crawled into, and go to see them: "You've always been a bit of a hermit, but now you should..." The calls were increasingly routine and full of impatience, a suppressed "you broke up, well, he left you, yes, which is worse, but no one has died." Impatience, even though she didn't complain, didn't talk about what had happened, didn't revel in her misfortune. Or perhaps for that very reason. Interest in other people's pain fizzles out at some point and eventually mutates into weariness. But denying people the chance to appear useful brought on instant weariness. She bored her friends. Her placid resignation was boring. That's why they rummaged, probed the crack through which something might escape: anger, contempt, or overt sadness, something to react to. Add some hot or cold water as necessary. No one wants to be the one offering lukewarm water.

She was engulfed by a Sunday afternoon heaviness. She lay down on the bed. August was not going down without a fight. The grey stone floor of her terrace looked white. Like the dead grass on the field behind the row of white-trunked poplars. Nothing but white, and the excruciating blue of the sky. Hot air. Cicadas. The fan rotated rhythmically to their song. She dozed off.

As the sun was getting low in the sky, she stepped out into the meticulous streets of closed-up houses. She looked at the facades as if she had on those X-ray glasses kids used to buy for themselves by mail order. Savings and pocket money spent on X-ray glasses, or sea monsters that turned out to be tiny seahorses: "That's not a monster." "Are you sure? Have you ever looked closely at a seahorse? Forget about the name and look at it again." She didn't need the glasses; she was familiar with many of the interiors. People invited each other into their homes there, like they did in villages or provincial towns. During visits, the owners moved around like actors in an advertisement. The door closing on the last guest to leave was like a director calling "Cut!" Bodies untensed, shoulders relaxed again, and bellies were let out, then the domestic wars resumed, perennial and insidious, even if they seemed innocuous at first. Not much imagination was needed, just statistics. In one in five homes, an abuser; one in six, an alcoholic; one in seven, someone with depression... In one of these houses there were perhaps several of these scourges or all of them, plus a big garden.

She needed to rip off the scab of monotony, she needed to feel something, anything. Any feeling would do; even an unpleasant one.

Discomfort.

She crossed the development, reached the last inhabited block, and followed the tarmac road formerly used by trucks and heavy construction machines. The August sun had turned the dark surface soft and sticky like a liquorice bootlace beneath the soles of her sandals.

At night, the uninhabited blocks could look sinister; during the day, the reality was strikingly clear. Unlike abandoned old villages, it was impossible to find beauty in these ruins, in the unfinished brick and concrete structures, building materials strewn all over the place, weeds, rubbish, dirty surfaces daubed with sun-bleached graffiti, some of which the rain had caused to sag like old tattoos. Like stubborn Samsons, the plants were hefting open cracks in the floors and walls.

The fence that enclosed the buildings separated her from the chaos to her left, but it did not stop the smells from drifting out; a dank stench emanated from one of the blocks. She held her breath. Her grandmother used to call these knee-jerk reactions "neurasthenia". What a pity that word had fallen out of use. It had been replaced by more precise but far less pleasing ones.

What had made a comeback, however, were the old fears that had skipped a generation. Such as the panic caused by rusty nails hidden like rodents among the unfinished building work; nails and metal teeth that could tear a child's skin and infect them with tetanus. That was another term she thought belonged to times gone by, and yet it was used to keep the children from the development out of there. They were supposed to be countryside kids, but their parents had turned them into meek little house plants. They were only allowed out in the open air when there were enough adults keeping watch. One for each point on the compass.

She got to the end of the tarmac road, the end of the development. It was time for the tiny ritual that would lift her spirits. She approached the edge of the tarmac, stood on tiptoe, spread her arms out like a tightrope walker, took a deep breath, lifted her right leg, and slowly lowered it until she touched the ground with her toe. One, two, three seconds. She lifted it up before the piranhas or crocodiles of her childhood had time to open their jaws. Game over. She turned around and walked back to the inhabited zone, her heart pumping again.

In the front garden of the blue villa she saw Ernesto Royo leaning against a low part of the railings smoking a cigarette. He blew the smoke towards the street as if he was afraid of making the flowers pong.

Before she could wave to him, a reggaeton track started blaring out from the cream-coloured villa across the road. It was a highly unacceptable level of noise, especially in that heat. An angry shout cut it off abruptly. The song of the cicadas returned.

"Thank God!" said the lawyer, smiling, wagging his chin in the direction of the cream-coloured villa. "What a bloody racket!"

She nodded.

"Out for a walk?"

"Yes. Just stretching my legs a bit. I've spent the whole day at my computer..."

Was she justifying herself? Again?

But that wasn't the reason for the uneasy feeling she had as they were making small talk. A silhouette was moving behind the blinds of the upper window of the villa, behind the lawyer. His wife – Paula? – had forgotten to turn off the lamp which, at dusk, was already winning the battle against the sunlight. She was eavesdropping on the conversation. Having attended many neighbourhood parties, she knew smoking wasn't permitted in any of the houses. People went out to the garden or onto the balcony.

"We're bringing Paula's parents here," he said, stubbing out his cigarette in the ashtray he held in his other hand. A dented Cinzano ashtray, maybe stolen from a bar back when they were young and wild.

"You've got a big house."

"Not big enough."

As he delivered this line without a smile, she realised he wasn't making some hackneyed joke about in-laws.

She said goodbye, not wanting the conversation to make her feel numb again.

The sky was also clouding over. Perhaps a storm was coming.

A clap of thunder. The balcony curtains stirred. Come on, come on, come on. She got out of bed and looked outside.

At dusk, the eleven saplings in front of the house had swayed in the wind, watching the clouds roll by: Here we are, we're over here. Now, as if realising they'd invoked the rain too vehemently, the eleven poplars had become still. She shut all the windows and went out onto the balcony in her pyjamas.

A second clap of thunder and a heavy, viscous raindrop hit the back of her right hand.

Another clap of thunder. Third warning. Drops began pounding the ground like projectiles, throwing up the scent of dust. Afterwards, when the water drenched her hair and made her pyjamas cling to her body, she smelled of wet earth. She was shivering with cold but did not want to go inside.

The wind began to blow intensely. She held on to the slippery railing. She could no longer see the little trees. The force of the water made her close her eyes. She opened her mouth, raindrops on her teeth, on her tongue. A clap of thunder rolled into her belly. She screamed.

She felt the building move. If it carried on raining all night, if it carried on all of the next day, and the next, the water would seep beneath the foundations, lift up the house, and wash it away. Where to? To the coast. They would all end up at the coast, the houses, the park, the trees. They all had roots that were still too shallow.

Carry us away to the coast.

Get us out of here.

11

In the morning, still half asleep, he had to bail out the water that had come in through the windows before he could go out. The sky was still overcast, but the clouds didn't look as ferocious as the ones that had emptied out during the night.

He walked for several hours, without sitting down once; he wanted to see what the rain had done to the landscape he was already coming to know and recognise. The previously hard dusty earth had darkened and softened. The stones gave way beneath the soles of his shoes. The air was laden with humidity, as hot and heavy as a coastal town. He felt euphoric. He even began to sing quietly.

At dusk he returned to the development. He was crooning some old one-hit wonder to which he could only remember some of the words. He made up the missing bits by inventing rhymes, some more nonsensical than others. When he couldn't think of a word, he would stop to think and then continue walking when he had remembered it. He ambled along happily, totally engrossed, like a child who has stumbled on the perfect game. He finished the song, then sang it from beginning to end. He repeated it a second time, slightly louder. When he got to the end, he laughed. He sang it again even louder. He entered the uninhabited zone through one of the holes in the fence, being careful not to snag his shirt on any of the metal spikes. When he got to the first buildings, between the columns and the rubble, he invented a silly choreography to his summer pop song. He was giggling so much he had to stop, bend forward and rest his hands on his knees.

"Fantastic," said a voice behind him.

He swung round, startled.

A few metres away, leaning against a column of the first apartment block, a man was watching him. A small, wrinkly old man with a thick mop of tousled white hair. He was looking at him with curious little eyes and a roguish smile, hands stuffed into his jacket pockets.

"Who are you?"

The man came out of the building and approached to shake his hand.

"Matías. I live here. Who are you?"

"You live here?"

"Three streets from where you live."

"How do you know where I live?"

"I've been watching you ever since you arrived, because you walk around like you're the only one here, as if there aren't any dangerous people in this place."

He looked at the man and was unable to hide a smirk, which was not lost on this Matías fellow.

"I don't mean me. You were bloody lucky nobody else spotted you on your walks. There's a guy living in the block opposite the one you broke into first who's a bit of a nutter."

"A neighbour?"

"He lives with his wife on a floor without any other neighbours and he's lost the plot, totally paranoid. Made worse by the fact he's got a shotgun."

"How do you know?"

"I saw the barrel poking out between the blinds. And I imagine that back there, in the shadows, he'll be keeping a lookout so no one sneaks into the blocks. Come on, let's get inside." The old man pointed to the derelict structure from which he'd emerged.

Still disconcerted, he followed Matías's footsteps, slow and steady like an old mountain goat. He felt a growing apprehension. The whole time he'd been in Luján's apartment, it seems he'd been the prey, evading capture purely because the hunter had got distracted or fallen asleep. Thinking about this, he had an irrational sensation of being hit simultaneously in the chest and back.

They passed a block where the ground-floor walls had been erected. A barricade. He stepped sideways to get in behind it.

"No. You're better off not going in there." The old man grabbed his arm to stop him. "There's ghosts." He turned around again as if that was the end of the matter, and beckoned for him to follow.

They wound their way between the buildings, the exact route both of them would take in the following days. He didn't understand why they took this particular route, but he accepted the old man's authority since he'd saved him from the barrel of a shotgun which, to tell the truth, he couldn't even be sure existed.

They arrived at the block where Matías lived.

"Coffee?"

"You've got coffee?" He'd run out two days ago but hadn't plucked up the courage to go and buy anything in town.

"Would I offer it to you if I didn't?"

They went inside and, despite his vertigo, he followed Matías up a staircase with no handrail to one of the third-floor apartments. The old man went inside after opening the padlock that held shut a door fashioned from planks of wood.

The first thing he noticed was the smell. A human smell. Sweat, breath, and food seeping into the open pores of the walls. The smell was more intense, pungent even, in a room like his where the windows looked out over the inner courtyard of the building. Beneath the window, a mattress covered with sheets pulled smooth and tight over it, like a hotel bed. There was a vegetable crate for a bedside table.

At the other end of the room he saw a gas stove, grimy kitchen utensils, and a pile of dishes of various colours and sizes. Plastic jerrycans filled with water, some tinned food, fruit that smelled too sweet. An insect flew past, too close to his eyes. Trousers, shirts, and sweaters hung over a wooden rack. The intense odour in the small, enclosed space began to slither up his nostrils, across the roof of his mouth and down, on its way to his lungs, but he didn't want to be rude to the man who was filling the coffee pot.

"Where did you—"

"From the petrol station. There's a Dominican guy who works there, he sells you whatever you need and doesn't ask questions. He also lets you use the staff toilet and showers. I don't go there to do my business, it's too far away. But you can't just do it wherever you want, like animals. I know how to dig a latrine, boy." He sounded like John Wayne.

"How come?"

"Ten years in the Blue Helmets."

"Where?"

"Here and there. It's on the ground floor of the building next door, because, although I put lime in it, naturally it's going to stink over time. There's no shortage of lime, as you can imagine. If you want to use it…"

He nodded, still dumbfounded by the whole encounter. The pot began to bubble over, the scent of coffee masking the various other smells.

Matías picked up two white mugs. One had rings on it from previous use. He handed him another one, which was full of dust.

"I don't usually have guests," joked the old man as he poured out the coffee, dissolving the dust. "Do you want sugar? There's no milk; it goes off quickly."

He said no, and waited, holding the mug.

"Come," said Matías.

They went into what was supposed to be the living room. The three openings to the street were covered with plastic strung up with ropes. The old man pulled aside the middle one, a shower curtain depicting Ariel from Disney's *The Little Mermaid*, which hung across the balcony with no railing. Several crooked towers of books were stacked against the opposite wall; next to them, a row of three chairs. Matías positioned two of the chairs to face the outside, then drew back two more tarpaulins to reveal glassless windows. He sat down facing Matías but moved his seat back slightly from the balcony, which felt to him like a diving board jutting out from the building. He shimmied his chair round even more, so he wouldn't be tempted to dive off. Before he took his first sip of coffee, he held the mug still in the air, hoping the dust would settle at the bottom again. He would have to sip it like Turkish coffee. When he finished, the dregs of dust and coffee at the bottom would reveal his future.

"So tell me, what brought you here?"

The old man had no way of knowing who he was or why he was in hiding, but the question was an intense reminder of it. He was scared his facial expression would give away the fact that he was a fugitive, or that the man wouldn't believe any story he invented. So he opted for an evasive approach.

"It's complicated. What about you?"

"Very simple for me. Running away from my children and from an old people's home."

"Won't they be looking for you?"

"I suppose so, but I don't think it would occur to them to look here." He laughed. He set down the mug and turned his head towards the balcony.

They both looked at the building opposite, from which they were separated by an untarmacked road and imaginary pavements. It mirrored his own: balconies without railings, empty window frames revealing bare walls and floors. After a while, Matías's breathing became deeper and slower; he had fallen asleep. He took a final sip of coffee without tilting the mug too much, then stood up.

The creaking of the chair woke the old man. "You not finishing that?"

"No. I have to go."

"Pass me your mug."

He held it out, and the old man drank it down in one gulp, dregs, future, and all. He was ashamed to have wasted the coffee out of squeamishness.

"See you around," said Matías, and turned back towards the balcony.

He left the apartment and started walking down the stairs, sticking close to the wall. Suddenly, the old man's voice drifted down to him: "Careful they don't see you. And if you want a shower, the Dominican is on night shifts every day except Sunday."

When he reached the street he looked up towards Matías's balcony. It dawned on him that the old man had not asked his name.

12

After the storm and several days of intermittent rain, everything changed colour, as if a pair of giant hands had flipped over the ochre fields to reveal the green meadows on the other side. Life had been crouching, waiting; in a matter of hours, thousands of green shoots had pierced the hard, rough earth. She would have loved to go on a long walk; she would have confronted her fear of the nothingness now it had all turned green.

That particular Friday evening, however, she'd been invited to a barbecue in one of the large villas, the white one with the door and window frames in Grecian blue.

"You have to enjoy the coolness, the fresh air, the night-time, the nature," the hosts kept saying.

Maite and Rodrigo were in their forties, co-owned a travel agency, and their children were away in Ireland learning English for the summer. They'd brought chairs and tables outside into their perfectly landscaped garden, which was resplendent after the rain. They had just returned from a fortnight's holiday in Italy and could not stop saying how glad they were to be "home".

Enjoy it.

She also had to enjoy herself, although she was always the one who could never be bothered to go to parties. Her ex-husband was the pleasant one, the sociable one, the witty one, the life and soul of the party. The one who wasn't there.

Enjoy it.

She would talk enthusiastically about the upcoming party, about the tombola, she would participate in everything. She would drink, would eat, would laugh. She wasn't going to make them feel sorry for her. She didn't feel sorry for herself either.

Enjoy it.

The guests had to enjoy the barbecue, the drinks, the desserts. They had to enjoy the garden games. They had to enjoy the conversations.

Everyone tried hard at this until the booze made explicit expressions of amusement unnecessary; the "how delicious", "how fun", "how funny", "how brilliant" gave way to less articulate but more authentic exclamations. They ate, they played games, they genuinely flirted.

Maite, who was lounging on a sunbed, gin and tonic in hand, suddenly shrieked and sat bolt upright. Splashes of drink darkened her blue blouse.

"What's wrong?" Rodrigo, beige Bermuda shorts, dark-green polo shirt, approached with a pétanque ball, black as a cannonball, in his hand.

"There's someone behind the hedge."

"A neighbour."

"But he's just standing there, peering through that hole." Maite pointed to the only area where there was a gap in the leaves.

"A nosy neighbour then." Rodrigo tossed the ball up in the air and caught it, several times.

Everyone was listening to the conversation. Someone had pressed pause on the party.

"But he looked weird."

"Come off it, Maite." Rodrigo clutched the ball, eager to get back to the game. "How can you tell from an eye peeping through a hole?" He made a circle with the thumb and forefinger of his free hand and held it up in front of his left eye. "What face am I pulling?"

Maite, all eyes on her, couldn't find an answer and was beginning to feel humiliated, so, still on her lounger, she adjusted her sunglasses, raised the gin and tonic as if toasting herself, and said, "You look like a one-eyed owl who's caught a pétanque ball thinking it was a rat."

Everyone laughed so hard that even Rodrigo had to laugh. He and Maite would talk about it later, if they remembered, after the guests had gone.

Before long, the volume of the voices and laughter returned to its previous level, but every now and then she glanced uneasily at the hole in the hedge.

13

He was no longer embarrassed to sing, but he discovered that he didn't know the words to many songs, so he started whistling. When was the last time he'd whistled? He remembered melodies well, so he could keep himself entertained for hours, repeating the same song and adding variations to it. The snippets of words, almost always the chorus, were added inside his head.

Despite how far he'd travelled during the day, that night he wasn't tired enough to sleep. He went for a walk around the streets of the zone. He was on constant alert, listening for sounds that would give away the presence of others and careful not to give away his own.

The appearance of a silhouette on a corner made him stop dead. He stepped inside a doorway, pressed up against the hole where the buzzers of the intercom should have been; he could hear them going off in his head like an inappropriate, childish prank. Suddenly, music. It was getting closer. Even if it was futile, he pressed himself closer against the wall. Some part of his mind tried to identify the song while his body tensed its muscles and braced its fists. But the man, younger than him, walked past the doorway without seeing him, his eyes fixed on the phone playing the music. It was getting quieter. When the song finished, the man played it again. Each time it came from further and further away.

He unclenched his fists when he could no longer hear it, and started to whistle softly, to see if he could remember the name of the song. He stepped out of the doorway. He walked past the block where the old man lived. The gate was open. He went in. As he'd forgotten his torch, he groped his way blindly through the lobby. "Matías!" he shouted up the stairwell.

Slowly, keeping his back pressed against the wall, he started up the steps in complete darkness. Perhaps it was better not to have the torch, not to see that the handrail was missing. He called out to the old man again.

"Up here!"

The voice came to him not from the apartment where the old man lived but from higher up, from the roof. If only he could close his eyes and ascend like a blind mountaineer. At the top, he was guided by a tiny reddish glow, the tip of a cigarette. Matías was sitting on a plastic folding chair with his feet resting on the railing, looking up at the structures that merged into the blackness of the fields. Next to him was a metal drum, which, judging by the smell, must have been used for a fire.

"Grab yourself a chair. There's more. They must have belonged to the builders who worked on this block, for when they had their lunch break." Matías pointed to where they were. "Want one?" The old man offered him a cigarette as soon as he sat down beside him.

In the flicker of the lighter, he could see Matías was wearing a shirt and tie.

"You look very smart."

"Well, I think it's someone's birthday today. I don't know whether it's mine or my wife's. Although, the way I'm feeling" – he placed his right hand on his heart – "I think it must be her birthday."

He leaned back in his chair and imitated Matías, resting his feet on the railing too. They smoked their cigarettes in silence.

The old man opened the military bag next to the chair and pulled out a bottle of rum.

"Where did you get that?"

"From the petrol station. I told you, you can get everything you need at the petrol station. He even lent me a shovel to bury my wife."

14

On Monday, when she checked her inbox, she found an email calling for an urgent meeting of the residents' association. Just one item on the agenda: the "incident" at the barbecue. She had forgotten about it; apparently others had not.

She went out for a walk. The pot-bellied clouds of the previous day had frayed, as if a giant rake had passed over them. The sky was streaked with shreds of white, too thin to yield any rain.

But they had left behind a hefty deposit of humidity. The ground sunk pleasantly beneath her feet as she walked around the development on her way to the park. The gardener had not yet done his rounds to repair the damage, and there were broken branches in some of the hedges. The stiff white body of an earthworm floated in a puddle.

Beyond the small, landscaped area, the land was taken over by scrubby bushes. Behind one of them she could make out the figure of a woman bending down and straightening up again, as if harvesting something. She was carrying a wicker basket over her left arm, filling it with whatever she was picking up from the ground. When the woman stood up again, she recognised the blonde hair and slender figure of Natalia, the wife of Sergio "don't call me chairman" Morales. She got closer, curious to see what she was picking up.

Hearing her footsteps, Natalia turned around. She was, as always, perfectly coiffed and made-up. She could see it then: she was picking up stones. The basket was almost full. "I'm done for the day," Natalia said, ignoring her quizzical expression. "Would you like a coffee?"

Natalia set off towards her own house, and she followed. She didn't know how to ask; or rather what to ask.

The other woman opened the garden gate and walked towards one of the two garages. She opened it. At the back, behind the car, were piles of wooden fruit crates filled with stones. "They're my prisoners." She dumped the contents of the basket into one of the crates, then swiftly closed the garage door, as if she feared they might escape.

They went inside the house, which smelled of vanilla. As if they had coordinated – and perhaps they had – every villa had a different air freshener. Roses in one, citrus in another, something that purported to be jasmine in another, or one of those sickly-sweet aromas used in clothes shops in the capital to try to mask the stench of the thirsty sewers and the customers' sweat. No one would try on clothes if they could detect the smell of the other customers.

The windows were closed. The cloying vanilla fragrance wafted straight up her nose, to her temples. They went into the kitchen, and while Natalia was concentrating on the coffee machine, back turned, she opened one of the windows. She took a deep breath to ease the encroaching headache.

"There can't be an infinite number of them," said Natalia, with the coffee grinder going in the background. "There can't be an infinite number of anything. Only numbers, right?"

Natalia was appealing to her authority as an IT person. It wasn't a question, it was a plea: tell me that's how it is.

"That's right."

A click, then the coffee started to flow out of the two valves.

"Before, when I used to find those stones in the park, I'd pick them up and throw them into the field. But the bastards kept coming back."

"They came back?"

"Yes."

"How could you tell they were the same ones?"

"Because I marked them with a blue felt tip before I threw them. A few days later, they'd be back in the park again. So now I take them prisoner instead."

Natalia held out the cup. Her hands shook slightly. They sat down to drink their coffee. On the kitchen counter, for all the world to see, lay boxes of medication that explained her stiffness, her trembling. The doctor in town had another valued customer in Natalia.

Two voices came from the first floor. Judging by the way they were talking, the boys were gaming on the computer.

"They wear headphones to listen to the other people they play against. I wish I could put them on mute too. And tonight we've got the residents' association meeting here."

Natalia reeled off all the things she was going to make. She didn't know if the other woman was simply telling her, or if she was expecting her approval, or some critical remark.

"Sounds good," she said.

"Really? Does it sound okay to you? Do you think we should have something sweet too?"

Natalia pushed her cup of coffee aside – she'd only taken a couple of sips – then got up and started opening and closing drawers and pulling out utensils. She placed some of them on the counter. With her body half concealed behind a cupboard door, her voice sounded far away, as if the cupboard was the opening to a tunnel.

"Maybe I should make a cake? Or perhaps brownies might be better?"

Even with the window open, the vanilla smell was unbearable. She finished her coffee in one gulp and said, "I'll let you get on."

Natalia poked her head out of the cupboard. "No, if I don't... it's really no trouble... Okay. See you tonight."

When she stepped outside the house she felt heavy and fuzzy-headed, as if the coffee had drunk her. In front of the garage, she saw a stone lying on the ground. It must have fallen out of the basket. Or escaped. She bent down to pick it up and looked back in case Natalia was watching her from the window, but she must have been deep inside the kitchen cupboards or the two-door fridge. She took the stone. It had sharp edges and was marked with a thick line of blue felt tip.

15

That night he went with Matías to the petrol station.

While he waited in the shadows, Matías did the shopping. Twenty euros in tips later, ten per head, the Dominican shop assistant disconnected the security cameras to allow them to enter the staff area and take a shower. First, Matías, who took no time, like an animal taking a dip in a watering hole, and then put on the same clothes he'd been wearing before. He savoured it for a little longer; he'd missed feeling warm water on his skin. Before putting on the clean clothes he'd brought with him in a bag, he defogged the rust-stained mirror with his dirty shirt. It was the first time he'd seen himself since leaving Luján's apartment. He was thinner, his skin browner. His grey hair had lightened in the sun. He took a pair of scissors out of the bag. He didn't shave, the beard concealed his identity better, but he trimmed it so he looked less like a tramp, or a prophet.

"I've got enough money for us to shower as often as we

want," he said as they made their way back across country. An arrogant brag that he regretted as soon as he'd finished the sentence.

"Let's not tempt fate. And anyway, we've got good ventilation," was Matías's argument. "And I don't want to know why you've got so much money. One of the great things about living here is that we can stop telling lies to each other. For me, you begin here."

And so he would carry on washing himself every day in the block's underground car park. He also washed his clothes down there and hung them up in the house. He had enough coffee, food, and cigarettes to last the next few days.

They arrived at Matías's place and went up to the roof.

"I'd like to know something—" he started to say.

"What happened to my wife? Is that it? It's written all over your face," said Matías, although he couldn't tell what look he was giving him. "Don't worry, I didn't do anything to her. She died. In fact that's why we came here, so she could die peacefully." His voice faltered and he took a deep breath. "We ran away from home like two silly teenagers. How about that?"

The old man lit a cigarette, and he did too.

"She planned everything, even the morphine for the end, and I followed her, as I've always done. Coming here was her idea, she knew some of the people living in the villas, I think. Yes, it was her idea. My whole life has been her idea. She died after a month and a half," he said, after taking a couple of puffs. "In hospital she would have done it a little later, but she'd have been unconscious and hooked up to all those beeping machines. She was so sensitive to noise that she couldn't even stand bells or horns. She once threw my radio out of the window because I'd been listening to it badly tuned for several minutes. 'Bloody piece of junk!'"

Matías threw the cigarette butt into the street in a wide arc and started laughing. Or crying, perhaps. The sound was muffled.

He was too curious not to ask. "Where's she buried?"

"Over there." Matías pointed towards the area of open wasteland at the end of the development. "Not because she was particularly fond of the place or anything. But the soil is softer there. These arms aren't what they used to be." He slapped his right bicep. "I get the impression she isn't best pleased, because she often visits me at night but doesn't say a word to me."

More out of awkwardness than anything else, he asked, "What if you took her some flowers?"

"They'd draw attention."

"Not if you plant them."

"They'd need watering."

"So water them."

Matías lit another cigarette.

"What was her name?"

"Teresa. The Dominican lent me a wheelbarrow, as well as a shovel." The memory was clearly distressing for Matías. "Although I never told him what I needed them for."

The old man fell silent, gazing in the direction of where his wife must have been buried. He didn't say anything else.

When he realised Matías had fallen asleep, he left. He took the stairs down extremely slowly. As he reached the street, he realised Matías had not asked him his name that time either.

16

The residents' association meeting had taken on a tone somewhere between grandiose and grim. It had wiped the smile off the face of Yolanda Vivancos, who, despite there being only one item on the agenda, had turned up with the folder of proposals for the Wine and Harvest Festival clutched to her chest like a giddy schoolgirl.

"Now is not the time," said Sergio Morales, more chairmanlike than ever, looking at her with a dismayed expression.

Sergio Morales was sitting directly opposite Yolanda Vivancos on one of the long leather sofas around the glass table covered with trays of snacks. Tiny cups, spoons, saucers, an army of miniature items laid out with military precision which nobody dared disrupt. Especially given the gravity of the chairman's voice.

"Now is not the time."

Yolanda Vivancos propped the thick folder against the side of the sofa she was sharing with two other residents' association members. Then her hands were freed up and began to hover over a row of mini slices of toast topped with lentil hummus and fresh goat's cheese. The left stayed in the air while the right swooped down with hawklike precision and carried one off. An opening at last. Everyone else leaned in, picking up a piece and bringing it to their mouths.

She chose a ramekin of ceviche. As she was in charge of writing the notes, with her laptop on her knees, she had the privilege of occupying a seat.

Natalia, the hostess, seemed pleased to see pieces missing from all the trays. Nobody there knew she was keeping hundreds of stones in captivity.

Morales waved his empty spoon in the air and reminded them of the purpose of the meeting. "He was one of those illegals. The more I think about it, the more I'm sure. None of us would ever have done something like that, openly snooping in someone else's garden."

"Let's stay focused," said Ernesto Royo, finishing off a little cup of strawberry gazpacho. "All Maite saw was an eye."

But the chairman ignored his comment. Germán, the only residents' association member who lived in a Phase 3 apartment, grunted.

She wasn't sure what the others thought of this resident, whether they saw him as an interloper to be tolerated or as an exotic plant to be cared for. In any case, he would be a carnivorous plant.

Germán, sitting next to Morales, put a little plate down on the table, rested his hairy hands on his thighs, and looked around, before saying, "I didn't want to say anything, so as not to alarm you, but a few weeks ago I thought I saw a stranger going in and out of the block opposite. I was about to do something."

"Do something?" she said, looking up from the laptop where she was noting down the names of the meeting's participants. "You weren't going to shoot him, were you?" Everyone knew Germán had a gun.

"Of course not. I was simply showing him what's what."

"Why didn't you?" she asked.

She was irritated by this roughneck act of his. He'd already told them, over beers and jokes, that he came from a very small town, the kind of place where any problems end up as pig feed – "If you catch my drift?" Germán also seemed to think that because he lived on the outskirts of the development he was defending a border post.

"Because he was well dressed. He didn't look like one of those down-and-outs... I thought he must be a visitor."

"What if he hadn't been well dressed? Just a warning shot?"

Her ex-husband used to criticise her for being too direct, even slightly "asocial", a word that almost sounded funny while they were in love with each other and became a reproach when they no longer were.

It took a little too long for Germán to say no.

"Please don't put that in the minutes," said Morales.

"Anyway, he must have left by now, because I haven't seen him since."

"Have you asked the people in that block if they had any visitors?" said Natalia before heading into the kitchen.

Germán looked at the floor.

She was about to make a scathing comment, but the hostess returned from the kitchen and filled their mouths with crostini topped with fish pâté. "I get it delivered from a deli in Santander. You must try it."

Everyone chewed in silence, but something inside Germán had been set in motion and would not be halted by the crunching of canapés. "We can't just go on being so passive," he said, after noisily cleaning the creamy remnants from his gums with his tongue. "If we don't do something, there'll be more and more of them."

"That's something for the police to deal with," Ernesto Royo replied.

"And what will the locals think?"

"You reckon they don't know?"

"I don't think so. They don't come out here."

"But one day the word will get out that we're infested. The best thing to do with a blight is to nip it in the bud. We have to find them and get them out of there. If we take them by surprise, I don't think they'll even put up much resistance. If we showed up in the early hours of the morning, while they're sleeping…"

Only one head – the gardener's – seemed to nod in approval at the proposal, but noticing everyone else's opposition, he wasn't as vehement as Germán.

"I'm sure Don Fernando—" the gardener began to say, but Sergio Morales interrupted him.

"Going in at dawn? Like Franco's secret police? Is that really how you want us to behave?"

The Charles Bronson of the development had no choice but to counter-attack: "Don't you know what the 'pull effect' is? These people are organised. They have a warning system. They're like bees, the first ones observe and then let the rest know where the food is, then they all show up..."

The veins bulged in her temples, her jaw clenched, her fists even more, but she couldn't stop herself from launching a kamikaze attack: "You're not honestly trying to explain it to us with bees and pollination? Aren't you a little off-topic?"

This was met with several nervous guffaws.

Germán turned to her, hands gripping his thighs. She had never felt so hated so suddenly. She almost shielded her face with the laptop.

Yolanda Vivancos's trembling voice cut through the steely atmosphere. "How about we stop all this unpleasantness and just focus on the preparations for the party?"

This time Sergio Morales didn't say "now is not the time", but they did have to wait for the sound of Germán slamming the door to stop ringing in their ears, before they carried on.

"Excellent ceviche. What's it made with?"

"Sea bass."

17

He spent the next four days away, exploring the surrounding area. He avoided roads, followed dirt tracks or went cross-country, without seeing a single person. Two of the nights he slept in solitary abandoned houses, where there were signs he wasn't the first to do so; perhaps that's why he felt safer sleeping out in the open or in a grove of trees that had a stream running through it, which seemed as out of place as the river of silver paper in the nativity scene on top of the chest of drawers at his parents' house. He woke with his clothes damp from the dew. Autumn was approaching slowly, nocturnally. The first rays of the sun chased it away, but it returned with the tenacity of the timid.

The concept of time dissolved; the days became as wide open as the space. His body, arms, chest, and lungs seemed to have expanded as well.

Coming back, however, the development looked much smaller to him. The silhouettes of the apartment blocks rose up in the middle of nowhere as if teeth, many of them decaying, had pierced the earth.

He had barely noticed the omnipresent crickets on his walkabout, but as he got closer to the buildings the noise intensified. He remembered the way he had recklessly broken in to Luján's apartment. That seemed like so long ago. How many days had it been? A month, give or take.

Slipping through a gap in the fence, he entered the zone filled with empty apartments. Suddenly he heard a faint sound. He stopped. Pieces of wood knocking against each other and a little voice humming. He darted down a half-paved street, dodged a cement mixer with the hungry mouth of a pterodactyl chick waiting for its parents to return with food, and peered through the doorway behind it. He saw the skinny back of a boy kneeling down, stacking wooden building blocks. A wobbly three-storey tower made with extra pieces of brick and tiles. The boy was so engrossed that he didn't notice him. Carefully, precisely, on the top of the precarious tower he balanced a little doll with golden hair and only one arm. He sat back on his heels to observe his work, then picked up a red ball and hurled it at the construction. The wood crashed down onto the concrete, making a sound like an out-of-tune xylophone. "Boom!" cried the boy, laughing uproariously.

"Hello, where did you come from?"

The boy turned and jumped to his feet. He did not smile back. He blinked a couple of times, and with a circular motion of his foot moved the pieces around on the floor as if erasing the traces of a crime. He can't have been more than six years old and he was gawky-looking only because, like puppies, he had disproportionately big feet, half covered by trainers with the toes cut off to fit. This must have been done recently, because in contrast to his arms and face darkened by the sun, his toes were as pale as worms.

"What are you doing here? Are you alone?"

Just then, he heard a woman's voice. The boy turned and strolled off in the direction of the voice. He didn't take anything with him, not even the little pieces of wood or the one-armed doll. Either he didn't care about them, or he didn't think they'd be useful to him. The shout came again, and the boy walked a little faster. He still did not understand what was being shouted; he could not make out whether it was an order or the child's name. Maybe both. The child disappeared inside a building. Everything went quiet again. In the distance, the crickets.

He went to find Matías.

The plank door of the apartment was padlocked shut. He found him up on the roof of the block. Looking out over the railing, hands clasped behind his back.

"Matías."

Matías did not move. He called him again. The old man turned like someone hearing a noise, rather than his name being called. He looked at him oddly, as if he were a stranger.

"Matías? It's me."

"You came back!" It seemed as if he hadn't expected him to come back, that he had written him off while he was away. "How many days have you been gone?"

"Four."

"How was it out there, in the big wide world?" The old man unclasped his hands and gave him an air hug. He was pleased he'd come back. He offered him one of the folding chairs.

They sat down. He put his rucksack down on the floor.

"Matías, I saw a little boy in one of the empty apartments."

The old man didn't respond, apparently more interested in the bird that had perched on the terrace railing of the building opposite and was watching them. It looked like some kind of hawk.

"The animals living here tolerate us. Don't mess with them. Don't kill mice or lizards or birds or spiders or insects. Here, they kill so they can eat. If you do it purely because they irritate you or disgust you, they'll get their revenge. A boy, you said? He's with that family who arrived the day before yesterday. They've set up in one of the ground-floor apartments at the back over there."

"So you know them? You've spoken to them?"

The old man nodded. The abundance of white hair buffeted by the wind looked like the plumage of a tropical bird.

"Just as I did with you. Every time someone arrives, I give them the once-over, to suss out who they are and what they're like. When you got here, there was already one couple who'd been occupying an apartment in Phase 2 for a few months. There are some Romanians in one of the first blocks in this part. Over there" – he pointed at some rooftops in the distance – "there are two more families, with animals and a vegetable garden. And over there, three young guys who I think are on the run. There aren't that many of us right now, but up to thirty people have come to live here. And most of them are like you and me, discreet and cautious, because although they don't know for sure, they imagine the residents on the development don't want us here."

"Do you know all of them?"

"All apart from one, who's a junkie. I don't think he'll last long here anyway. He's hiding out. Hiding out here is easy, but it's also hard to get certain things, if you catch my drift. You get these fly-by-nights who stay for a day or two and then leave. If you want, I'll introduce you to the family."

"Oh no... I don't know..."

"As you like. There's no hurry, is there? It's not like you're leaving tomorrow."

Until then, that possibility hadn't even crossed his mind.

18

"I must have thrown them away by accident when I was cleaning."

The look on the doctor's face showed she was in no way convinced by her excuse of losing the packet of pills, even though she'd thrown words like "tidying up", "cleaning", "fixing", and "work" into the story, the words doctors are supposed to like hearing before they sign off another prescription for anxiety meds. The doctor could have rejected the story with a simple "I'm not buying it", but she didn't seem to be in the mood for a confrontation. Perhaps because the preceding conversation had made it difficult. They'd been discussing literature. Few things could create greater complicity in that place. They were two educated women who talked about books, who were different from everyone else, who were readers, who were superior; although with an expert command of false modesty, they demonstrated this by pitying the non-readers. Non-reading patients in the doctor's case, and non-reading neighbours in hers: none of them knew what they were missing by not reading…

She would do whatever it took to get her hands on that prescription.

Finally, the doctor gave her the piece of paper with a weary look, leaving her slightly concerned that she'd tarnished a relationship which had its uses, sure, but which she also valued in its own right.

So, three days later, she decided to accidentally-on-purpose bump into the doctor. She went to pick up a parcel of books at the post office at the exact time the doctor visited the health centre. The post office was only a few metres away. She waited inside, pretending to check the parcel's contents, until she saw the doctor sluggishly getting out of her car. The doctor, also in her forties, had lost her waist a long time ago, although a braided red leather belt reminded her of where it had once been.

She went outside, to pretend to bump into her. "Look, doctor. What a haul!" she said, holding up the box.

"Ooh, books? How many?"

"I can't even remember. I ordered them from the bookshop a couple of weeks ago."

"If you read any good ones, pass them on to me, okay? I really trust your judgement."

She assured her she would, and walked away happy. Order had been restored to the world.

For the next few nights she did not take any pills at bedtime. She needed to give it a reasonable amount of time before going back to ask for another prescription. She read in bed until the book dropped onto her face; then she put it to one side, trying to move as little as possible, turned out the light, and willed herself to sleep. A few minutes later she realised she was still awake, as if, groping around in the dark, she'd been unable to find the door that led to sleep. She would turn on the light again, pick up the book, go back two or three paragraphs from where she had left off, and read for a while longer until the book was tilted dangerously close to her face. Again she put it down on her right-hand side, the side where he used to sleep. The position of the bedside lamp kept her in the place she had occupied when there were two of them.

She usually had to go through this process twice, although sometimes she needed to do it one more time.

Three nights without pills. She would have liked to hang a calendar up in the kitchen with a square for each day, so she could mark them off with a big red cross. Writing *NP* (no pill) on her phone calendar was not quite as satisfying.

On the fourth night, she woke up at sunrise.

When she went out onto the balcony, she saw a group of rats running through the fields.

"They're voles," said the gardener, whom she saw later that morning when she went out for her run. "They're not rats, but they're still a pest."

"But they haven't come into our domain."

"They know what's waiting for them if they do." He drove the blade of the shovel into the earth.

She said nothing. She knew she was under observation. She had to be on her best behaviour, so she sent Yolanda Vivancos a message telling her how many numbered raffle tickets she'd calculated they'd need to print for the tombola. She accompanied this with a detailed explanation, even including a couple of mathematical formulae. She wondered if she'd taken it a bit too far. But the reply seemed enthusiastic. A long email explaining how the preparations were going, and that the party logo would be printed on the tickets as soon as they'd decided on the design. After an insincere request to the other woman to keep her up to date, she set to work.

At midday, she saw the voles again. They zigzagged along like drunks, dazed by the sun. They seemed to be looking for something. Perhaps they had lived there before the development was built and were still looking for their burrows. The humans had failed to make their own nests, while the voles were searching for their lost nests. All displaced, all uprooted, because they hadn't managed to find a new place to live.

She dreamed about homeless rats. "They're voles," the gardener told her, and she caved his head in with a shovel.

The next night, she decided her period of abstinence was over. One Campari, with half a pill. *HP*, she noted on her phone.

Out on the balcony, she sat holding her glass, an ice cube and a slice of orange bobbing in it. Clouds covered the moon; different ones, not ones that brought rain, but ones that brought only darkness.

She poured herself a splash more Campari. The second time the ice did not crackle, no longer shocked by the change in temperature. She stretched out her legs and slumped down in the chair a little. Everyone must have been sleeping. She was alone with the crickets.

Or was she? There was something else out there. The landscape had changed. She sat up. She spotted a dark, swaying wall in the distance. It disappeared when she looked straight at it. It was visible again for a few seconds and faded away again, but then she could hear it. The sound of many trees shaking their branches, making them creak and rustle. There was no wind. And no trees either. These were the ghosts of the forest that had once stood on that land. Phantom trees. Why was she being allowed to see them? What had they come for? Apparitions always occur for a reason. Had they come looking for her? To warn her? About what? To chase her away? Where to?

She stood up, slightly weak at the knees, and approached the railing. She could not see much apart from her eleven saplings and the nothingness beyond. She downed her drink and tossed the remains of the melted ice out into the darkness. She shouted at the phantom forest, "Where are you? Why are you hiding? What's going to happen?"

19

He hadn't seen or spoken to anyone all day. He spent several hours lying on the cool floor of the apartment's living room, with a chipped plate resting on his belly as an ashtray. A thick spider's web shimmered in a corner. Staring at the stains on the ceiling, he lost himself in daydreams and memories.

In the evening he went out for a walk, as he had done in the early days. He felt light; there was a spring in his step. He did a circuit of most of the development and came to the roundabout at the entrance. He leaned his back against the wide post of Pacheco's *P* and felt how cold and hard the stone letter was against his back. The air was motionless, weighed down with the heat from the ground.

Just as he was dozing off, he heard the sound of an engine. He opened his eyes and saw the headlights of a car approaching. He hid behind the letters.

He expected the vehicle to go straight over the roundabout and head towards the houses, but the car didn't make it all the way round. It stopped before turning into the main avenue and did a careful parking manoeuvre, as if there were other cars around. The engine cut, then the headlights went out. Why was someone stopping right there? He didn't think the person driving had seen him; he was a shadow among shadows.

The car door opened. He crouched down even further behind the middle letters of the sign. A soft thud, then footsteps. Slow, hesitant footsteps that approached, bypassed the roundabout, and headed towards the adjoining park. He peeped out and saw a man walking alone. From the way he walked, he could tell the man wasn't young, but his walk was confident, self-assured, even though the only light came from the waning moon.

He looked over at the car. A top-of-the-range Mercedes, although not a current model. The man continued on his way. He was heading for the statue of the founder's grandfather. Approaching the pedestal, the silhouette slowed its pace, shoulders hunched, head down. He reached the foot of the statue and made a movement with his right arm, appearing to cross himself. Then the man sank to his knees and wept, face hidden in his hands. He cried with the desperation of children who have hurt themselves yet don't burst into tears until their parents arrive, then sob inconsolably because their teeth hurt from clenching so hard.

When the tears eased off, his voice could be heard, at first choked, then increasingly articulate. "I'm sorry... I'm sorry."

He realised the man in the Mercedes was the developer, Fernando Pacheco, whom everyone assumed had fled abroad, coming to apologise to his grandfather for his failure.

But statues aren't known for bending down to console people. At most they might pull themselves off the pedestal to punish a Don Juan.

20

The new moon made it impossible to see the phantom forest. However, she could hear it far in the distance. Leaves rustled and crackled as if they were on fire. Perhaps that was how the trees had died, burned in a fire. Burning down trees must have been an endemic problem, not just a symptom of the voracious boom years. She looked up at the starry, joyless sky.

Something tickled her arm. An ant, the scout. While the development slept, the industrious insects ceaselessly tunnelled away below ground. Tiny black cells that fought against them as if battling an infection. She blew the ant away.

At some point, the rowdy voices of unruly teenagers could be heard in the distance. School would start again soon. The full moon awakens the werewolf. Darkness brings the wolf out of the teenage boy. Poor little almost-human beasts.

She washed down the pill with another Campari. Was it true the red colour of the Italian bitter came from beetle chitin? That must be one stunning insect. Or simply ugly and red. You are what you eat, their grandmothers used to say, although their mothers' generation had already done away with that phrase. So she would grow a shell. Hopefully it would also be red, or black with red dots. She remembered "Circe", the short story by Cortázar in which a woman, Delia, one of those names that sound so good in an Argentine accent, makes hard-boiled sweets out of cockroach shells. She sucked a small piece of ice, crunched it with her teeth, toasting Delia and not Kafka, who never claimed to be a cockroach but a bug, and wondered whether yellow chartreuse must be made out of the goldbug. Stevenson? No. Poe. She was drunk, and the pill was already flowing happily through her veins, which were twice as red.

As she swirled the watery remains around the glass, one of the ice cubes bounced out of it and over the balcony railing. What if it landed on some poor bug that happened to be passing through the garden?

That night she fell asleep chuckling to herself at the image of a snail frozen in its little house.

"Attention, ladies and gentlemen. For the first time in the history of this discipline, our champion is going to play the perfect game, something never before achieved. How many times has she had us on tenterhooks, on the verge of witnessing this heroic feat? How many times has she come close? How many times has the tiniest mistake, a little oversight, caused her to lose all her hard-won gains? But today, ladies and gentlemen, today is the big day."

With her eyes closed, as the rules dictated, she bent down, reached into the laundry basket, felt the surface for the place to tug, and pulled out one of the damp garments. She stood up and opened her eyes. Good. Nothing had fallen on the floor. She stretched out the shirt. Pegs of the same colour and equidistant from each other. First rung of the clothes line, as she'd learned hanging out the laundry in the inner courtyard of her parents' house. Large neutral pieces in front; underwear bringing up the rear, out of sight of inquisitive windows.

"We continue, ladies and gentlemen. Another garment. We're one step closer to the perfect game."

She repeated the process. This time she hooked a sock. These were the enemies, the ones who hid between the clothes and fell on the ground. Splat! Game over. See you later, washerwoman. She hung it out. Its partner crouched in wait.

Another T-shirt. Trousers. Good. Everything was going well. That's it, slowly, a couple more garments. What if this time it went well? A pang. Fear? She yanked at the remaining clothes and, as she lifted up a blouse, the damp sound, like a frog hitting the windscreen. She opened her eyes. The other sock had fallen to the ground. Oh well.

"Uh-oh, bad luck! You've lost again. Maybe next time."

Exactly.

Next time. After the party. Tomorrow. And what would she do if she ever actually succeeded? Would she do the thing she'd half jokingly promised herself? She'd made a bet with herself. How embarrassing to delude yourself like that. What was the point? Nobody would be more willing to let you off than yourself.

It was only a game.

If that white car drives past me before I get to my front door, I'll die.

If I touch the railing while I'm climbing the stairs, I'll get an electric shock and die.

If I step on one of the red tiles in the corridor, I'll fall into a river of lava and die.

But if I play the perfect game, I'll leave.

It's a game; nothing ever happens.

Even if I have felt the breath of the rivers of lava in summer.

Perhaps one day an armada of voles in uniform will come to take over again. In uniform? But of course! Especially the ones on the front line. Onward, voles!

To be on the safe side, she hung up a pair of white knickers in plain sight.

21

For two days and nights he had avoided Matías. Suddenly the old man and all those people agitated him; they were a noise he couldn't block out.

He went back to the roundabout, but the Mercedes did not reappear. As the hours passed and he sat, smoking and daydreaming with his back against one of the stone letters, the memory of Pacheco became embellished with invented details in his mind: the steps towards the statue of his grandfather became slower, the crying more anguished, and the statue tilted its head and shook it disapprovingly.

The serenity of the previous days had disappeared, he said to himself, it had been an illusion. In the last inhabited zone there was an armed man stalking intruders. In the uninhabited zone there were the others, too many of them. For now there was a semblance of calm, but he imagined this was because the orbits of their planets had not yet intersected, and this could happen at any time. Then the conflicts would start, and conflicts meant the police would show up.

Therefore the sensible thing to do would be to pack his things into his rucksack and go somewhere else. But to his surprise, he had to admit he was reluctant to give up his refuge, his windowless apartment, his play kitchen propped against the wall, his bed made of stolen blankets, his guardian rat. He had to admit that the attachment didn't vanish if he exchanged those sentimental possessive pronouns for cold hard articles, because he did not want to give up the windowless apartment, or the stolen blankets, or the play kitchen. Or Matías.

The following day, he ran into the old man crossing a street a couple of blocks away, with his frail, jittery steps. He called out to him. Matías stopped to look at him. He was holding something in his arms, but with the light behind him, it was hard to make out what it was until he got closer. Two plants, two small shrubs with the roots exposed. "They bloom in spring," he said.

"Where did you get them from?"

"Last night, from a flower bed in the settlers' area."

"They'll notice."

"They'll think it was an animal of some kind. Will you come with me?"

As they crossed the dirt roads, he saw a knife, fork, and spoon sticking out of the old man's jacket pocket. "Are those your tools?"

"Afraid so, but if you help me we can do it quickly."

He looked at the length of the roots. "How deep is... she?"

"Don't worry, I dug deep. The other one's a little shallower, but we shouldn't run into him either."

He stopped in his tracks. Matías didn't seem to notice, or didn't want to. "What do you mean, the other one?"

"The other dead body." Matías quickened his pace, the cutlery clinking impatiently.

If he wanted to know more, he'd have to follow him. They were drawing level with a building that had no walls.

"Who's the other one?"

"A homeless man. Some poor sod." He took a deep breath before adding, "Those fly-by-nights are the most dangerous. That's why I've got the apartment all boarded up like that. They're prone to thieving and fighting. Luckily we don't get many of them passing through here. This place is so deserted it doesn't even have tramps. But every now and then one of them turns up, like him."

They left the built-up area and reached the wasteland where he'd arrived more than thirty days earlier. He looked for the mounds that would give away the graves. Only grass, alternating patches of green or dry grass.

"Are there more?"

"No, just Teresa and the tramp."

"What was his name?"

"I don't think I ever knew it, and the other guy didn't tell me either."

"What do you mean, the other guy?"

"The one who killed him."

"You're kidding me."

He trod on something soft and looked at the ground apprehensively. He lifted his foot. It was only green grass.

"I'm not in the habit of making jokes about dead people." Matías stopped abruptly, as if he'd reached the edge of a precipice, and added in a solemn tone, "They don't take kindly to it."

He placed the plants on the ground, took the cutlery out of his pocket, knelt, and started pulling up dry grass.

"Your wife?"

He stayed some distance away because he didn't know where the other one was. He could still feel the uneasiness in the sole of his foot.

"Yes. The other one's over there." Matías pointed to the right.

He approached the old man. "Leave that, I'll do it. Where do you want it?"

Matías marked a cross in the soil using the knife. He began to turn it over with his fork and used the spoon as a shovel.

A few minutes later the shrub was planted. As he patted the earth down with his hands, Matías had moved a few metres away and was marking out another cross. He dug there.

Matías, next to him, was gazing into the distance. "They showed up in November. Two men and a girl of about twelve. At first I avoided them because there was something about them that made me uneasy, but then I started going up to them, as if I was just one of the settlers taking a stroll. Nothing much, just a wave, a bit of a chat about where they came from and where they were headed, then I'd carry on my supposed walk."

He did that for a couple of days. He also showed them where to light a fire at night so it couldn't be seen from the other part of the development. He never let on that he was like them.

"They already had that predatory look of people who've been on the streets too long and see the rest of the world as potential loot. And there was something sinister about them as well. Full of pent-up anger, ready to explode. That's what happens when you're thrown together by circumstance. Sometimes it's best to go it alone."

One morning Matías found one of them wandering around between the blocks as if he was lost and couldn't find his way out. His clothes were even more torn than when he'd arrived and were stained with what he immediately recognised as blood.

"They'd had a fight, he said, because the other man had tried to rob him. I was about to leg it, but then the little girl appeared and took the man's hand. I realised the murderer was her father, and then I understood the real reason for the fight. So I went to the petrol station, asked the Dominican for the shovel, and that night we buried the other guy."

"And you didn't mind burying him next to your wife?"

"Why? She has her place, and that poor wretch has finally found his. And the land doesn't belong to anyone."

They planted the second shrub.

"Tonight I'll come and water them," said Matías as he dusted off his trousers.

When they reached the first strip of tarmac they looked back and contemplated their work. Matías had chosen the plants wisely; from a distance they were completely inconspicuous.

"Cup of coffee?" the old man asked once they were back at his apartment.

He didn't say anything about what he'd seen at the roundabout. Although the old man was also a fugitive and, therefore, like him, had no desire for anything to happen on the development, he thought it was wiser not to let anyone know about Fernando Pacheco showing up.

"It's always good to have a bit of company after a cemetery visit." Matías placed a steaming mug in his hands.

That night, Matías took him to meet the people who'd moved into the ground floor of one of the blocks, the little boy's family.

They were greeted by two men around his age and who must have been brothers, they looked so alike. One of them, who wore a suit waistcoat, was tending the fire over which they were heating some tinned food; the empty tins were being used by the boy to build a new tower. He was stacking them up along with pieces of brick and wood. Realising he was being watched, the boy looked him straight in the eye and knocked over the tower with a flick of his hand. He took this to mean that he had recognised him.

He also heard the woman's voice he'd heard before, but this time he could understand the words: "Stop making a mess, love."

Turning towards where the voice had come from, he saw a woman sitting at the table in a corner. She was a large woman, spilling over the edges of the chair, but she was far from flabby. A strongwoman from a travelling circus, stranded there after having her tent and elephants stolen in some dead-end town.

As his eyes grew accustomed to the feeble light coming from gas lamps and the flame of the stove, he could make out a few tatty armchairs positioned to resemble a living room; on one side were four mismatched chairs around a table; on the opposite side, the stove and a pile of pots and pans. The mattresses for sleeping on were in another room. Not everyone living in a precarious situation did so without baggage, without anything that might prevent them from getting moving again. Some people accumulated all kinds of objects in an attempt to build themselves a nest; they kept seeking a home in every dump with a roof they crawled into. The old man had told him they'd arrived in a van, prised open a section of the fence, squeezed through, and sealed it up again. The two men were labourers who'd been unemployed for years. He would have loved to know what she did for a living, but it was better not to ask questions and not to have to give answers either.

They sat down to eat. One of the men was the woman's husband, the other the child's father. The similarity of the two men, plus the lack of any signs of affection or resentment towards the woman or child, meant he couldn't remember who was who. Better that way. The issue of emotions was too dangerous. He needed to be more careful. He'd grown fond of Matías. The last thing they needed was this husband, wife, widowed brother-in-law, and orphaned child, he thought, with as much cynicism as he could muster. He left it to Matías to make conversation.

"Do you know how long you'll be staying?" Matías asked them.

"Not too much longer," said the man in the waistcoat. He served him a helping of ravioli with tomato sauce, on a green plastic plate. "The winter's tough here, and there's nothing to do."

He found out that they'd come to the development because they'd heard that construction was starting up again, and that they might find work.

"They always need workers like us in places like this," said the other man. "No contracts, no taxes."

"No questions asked, no rights. Like the ones straight off the boats, but with the language," said the woman.

Matías ignored the sarcasm. "Where will you go?"

"To the south, to the heat." The woman handed the child a plate.

"Doesn't he go to school?" he asked, pointing at the boy.

"What for?" she said. "He's a bit slow. We'll teach him whatever he needs to know, won't we?" She ruffled his mop of hair and the boy gave a contented grunt.

"If he wasn't," said the man in the waistcoat, "I'm sure he'd be an architect. He spends his days putting up little houses."

"And knocking them down," added the woman.

The ravioli tasted the same – it probably was the same – as the ravioli he'd eaten when he was young, on his first backpacking trips. The same texture, the same sweet, pungent flavour of the tomato sauce, a formula as secret as Coca-Cola. A one-dish meal. One of the first habits you leave behind when you step outside of society are meals in parts, you eat what you have, full stop, without any fuss or hierarchical way of dividing the foods into starters or mains. Dessert was a luxury one could only dream of under those circumstances.

"Slow down, kid." The woman slapped the boy on the back of the neck. "It's like feeding a little animal, he just never stops eating."

"Not that you can tell."

"Another of ours died. He wasn't like him."

"That was bad luck," said the other man.

He still couldn't tell which of the two men was the father.

The child carried on eating, oblivious. Sometimes it's better not to understand.

"Come on, little one, eat, eat." Another slap to the back of the head, this time gentler.

After finishing his meal, the child began to nod off. They laid him down on a mattress in the next room. Matías took the bottle out of his bag.

A while later, all of them relaxed and chatty from the rum, the man not wearing the waistcoat started telling a story.

"It happened to me when I was travelling along the Catalan coast. Before we met."

"So you're not brothers?" he asked.

The two men looked at each other before the man in the waistcoat said, "Brothers? Do we look like we are?"

He looked at them more closely. Beneath the weather-beaten skin, the close-cropped hair and shabby clothes, he now saw two very different people.

"We met in Seseña, in Toledo. We were working on the building sites before everything went to shit with the crisis. How long ago was that?" said the man in the waistcoat.

"Best not to think about that," the woman interrupted. "Carry on."

"Well, it was summer, and one night I went to sleep in an abandoned hotel in Sitges. On the first floor, because then you have time to hide or run away if anyone shows up unexpectedly. I went into one of the rooms that still had a roof, although there was no furniture in it and no doors or windows. In the morning, I walked around to see if I could find anything, and discovered a dead man on the first floor."

"Was that your first dead body?" Matías asked.

"No. But it was the first time I'd seen a young person

dead. The boy had been there for a couple of days. I got close enough to see that he still had a needle stuck in his arm."

"I found one like that once in Cartagena—" began the man in the waistcoat, but the woman asked him not to interrupt, so the other man could continue.

It was clear these stories had been told before, many times, and that night she wanted their guests to hear it for the first.

"His eyes were so blue, and wide open. I felt so bad leaving him lying there that I piled up some paper, wood, and grass at the other end of the building and set light to it."

"Like a Viking funeral pyre?" Matías asked. He was so engrossed in the story that his face had come alive again. His hair looked blonde in the yellowish light.

"No! It was so they'd see the smoke from the town and the police would find the body. Everyone deserves a dignified burial."

Matías, next to him, whispered in agreement. His eyes were watery.

They said goodbye shortly after that. Out in the night air, he realised he'd had too much to drink. Matías also moved with the stiffness and excessive caution of the carefully concealed drunk. He respected the old man's efforts to appear dignified, and so said nothing.

They were halted by a noise coming from inside the building to their left. "Don't stop here," whispered Matías. "It's the ghost block."

"What do you mean?" He had a vague recollection of him saying something about this, the day they met. "What ghosts?"

"They're the ghosts of two builders who died while working on this block."

Matías was serious. He didn't take his eyes off the building but his body was poised, ready to flee in the opposite direction.

"What are they doing here?"

"They're lost souls, because they died without finishing the work."

Although he was scared, he felt loosened up by the booze and let out a laugh.

"Don't laugh."

Voices and shouting coming from inside the block brought Matías to his knees in the street. He grabbed the old man's arm and noticed he was trembling beneath his coat. He pulled him to his feet.

"It's them! It's them!" Matías spluttered.

He tried to move him but the old man's body was rigid with terror. "Come on, Matías, move."

Laughter. More voices.

"They're coming closer."

Yes, they were coming. He gave the old man a push to get him out of there, to get him moving. Loud laughter, overlapping voices, the sound of footsteps and a bottle falling to the ground and smashing. Another nudge to get him behind a wall, before the gang of five teenagers could spot them.

They passed by, shouting, coughing, hitting each other, belching then laughing.

He waited until the voices were far away.

Matías was panting. "Stand back," the old man barked, then leaned against the wall with his hand and vomited. Ravioli with tomato sauce, rum and fear.

He accompanied Matías home, all the way up to his room to make sure he got there safely. The old man seemed slightly feverish.

"Are you feeling better, Matías?"

"Yep. But let's never mention this, okay?"

He promised.

The old man waved him away.

Making his way down the stairs was a struggle. No longer having to concentrate on helping Matías, he could once again feel the effects of the alcohol. He went down slowly, with awkward steps, knees giving way. He didn't switch on the torch, as that would make it worse.

The next day, the stiffness in his thigh muscles was worse than the hangover.

22

This time she did it in the morning. It was the weekend, and she had too many hours and not enough work. While the development slept or did their Saturday morning shopping, she needed her game. She wondered if, like addicts, she would start craving her hit sooner and sooner. She reached the road and started walking, her eyes fixed on the streets beyond the fence to her left that "protected" them from the uninhabited zone. They were afraid of the empty buildings, and even more afraid if there were people occupying them. Her included. She quickened her pace when she saw a hole in the fence. Not because someone might have got in, but in case someone happened to be lurking around at that moment.

On her way back, there was a transition from sadness to uneasiness, and from uneasiness to fear. The sadness was brought on by the buildings that were almost finished; she could feel the disappointment in that *almost*. They could not be described as abandoned buildings, like the next ones, because they had never been lived in.

In the distance, in the middle of the open countryside, she spotted a white shape that wasn't there last time she went past: a small fridge, dumped, stranded like a tortoise on its back. A dead tortoise. If she opened the door, the stench of its rotting entrails would be released along with the ghosts of all the iceberg lettuces that languished abandoned at the bottom of the vegetable drawer, hidden by the tomatoes.

She left the carcass behind and carried on to the end of the road.

The weeds continued their ceaseless tunnelling. Vegetable piranhas devouring the tarmac millimetre by millimetre. How thick was the layer of tarmac between her and the actual earth? Seven or eight centimetres. She peered over the edge as if looking into an abyss, a grey cliff with waves of dry grass crashing against it. Down. Far, far down. Vertigo. Eight centimetres of vertigo. She crouched down slowly, afraid of falling. "I'm not fainting, I'm controlling my movements." First in a downward-dog position. "Undignified." The flower-printed dress covered her like a tablecloth. She lowered her knees to the ground until she was on all fours. She lifted her head up, looking for a spot to focus on to overcome the dizziness, but the landscape offered only flat surfaces and the dark ribbon of road, the promised land, black tarmac, distant and unreachable. She sat back on her heels. She imagined herself catatonic, waiting months, years, for the advancing weeds to reach her with glacial slowness.

A sound snapped her out of it, something brushing against something else. A rustle. She looked up, expecting to see the silhouette of a crow or a magpie. The sky was completely empty. Out of the corner of her eye, she saw something move, and she turned her head. A tall man with grey hair was looking at her, leaning against the lone wall of one of the unfinished blocks. "One of them."

She sat up and smiled at him. He smiled back and gave what appeared to be an apologetic shrug. Then he turned and disappeared, as if the building had swallowed him up.

She ran back towards the inhabited zone.

23

He let Matías sleep until midday even though he urgently needed to talk to him. He found him still lying on the mattress but awake. As promised, they did not mention what had happened the previous night, but the old man sat up to tell him about the dead man with the blue eyes, in Sitges.

"I dreamed about him, I almost saw him."

"The man described him pretty well." He sat down on the floor at Matías's feet.

"But did he mention that the needle was stuck in his right arm?"

"Not that I can remember."

"So how come I saw it?"

"A fifty–fifty guess."

"But that would mean he was left-handed."

"Or he'd run out of healthy veins in his left arm." He had seen many junkies, dead and alive, over the years.

Matías gave him an inquisitive look. At that moment he was wondering about his past. "Why did you come to visit me?" he asked instead.

"To remind you that you need a haircut. Come on, out of bed, I'll tidy you up a bit."

Matías threw off the blankets. He had sweated out the alcohol and the remaining fear under a thick layer of them. Contrary to the old man's prediction, he hadn't yet become accustomed to certain smells, so he stood up and made coffee on the stove while Matías got dressed without washing. He cleaned himself every day. Although he'd escaped in a hurry, he had taken shampoo, toothpaste, and a bar of soap with him. The Dominican at the petrol station had promised to get supplies for him. "I'll go to the supermarket for you, bro."

He washed his clothes with the same soap. Everything smelled of Heno de Pravia. He'd given a piece to Matías, who sometimes used it, but he had not done so for several days. With the coffee slightly masking the old man's odour, he placed one of the chairs at a safe distance from the balcony. Matías sat up very straight, eyes closed, while he had his hair cut.

Snip, snip, snip.

The cuttings fell onto the tiles of their makeshift barber's. Only half the floor surface was tiled. Had the tiles run out, or had the labourer quit when he found out he would never get paid for the job?

Snip, snip, snip.

"You know the others?"

"Which others?"

"The settlers."

"I've seen a fair few of them, why?"

"This morning, I saw a woman walking around here—"

"The one with the schoolmistress glasses? Who only ever goes as far as the end of the tarmac road?"

Matías told him that the woman lived in a terraced house at the end of the inhabited zone, that she appeared to live alone, and that from time to time she took walks round there.

"She always does the same walk, touches the ground with one toe, and then turns back."

Matías began to talk to him about the other settlers, but he wasn't paying much attention; in his mind he took off the woman's shoes and she dipped her toe into a sea of grass. And did not run away.

Just then, Matías reached into his bag and pulled out a small battery-operated radio. "Look what the Dominican gave me," he said, and switched it on. The air was filled with voices from another world.

"Turn that off." His voice was as sharp as the scissors he was holding. Matías obeyed instantly.

If they were still looking for him, which they were, they wouldn't announce it on the radio. His disappearance and the reasons for it were not information that would be made public. The people tracking him down would be doing it in secret. It wasn't that. It was because he didn't want to know what was going on in the world outside that place. That was all. He longed for the day when he could no longer say for certain how many days he'd been there, when there was only the here and now.

"All done." He brushed a few hairs off Matías's shoulders.

"What a pity I haven't got a mirror! Maybe tonight I'll go to the petrol station…"

"I'll go with you."

"But we showered three days ago. It's not shower day."

"Perhaps it is."

When he left the petrol station, he was clean and wide awake. He accompanied Matías through the dark fields and dropped him off at the entrance to the block. Then he walked away as if he was going to his own block but instead cut back into the land surrounding the houses. He walked as far as the inhabited zone. He approached the final houses, where Matías had said the woman lived. The streets in that area were extremely well lit. He hoped his tidy appearance would help him avoid suspicion if some resident, also wide awake, happened to see him passing by. He came to two terraced houses with gardens. Both were in darkness. One looked uninhabited; the other had to be the one Matías had told him about.

He patted his jacket pockets. The cigarettes gave him an excuse to stop. He lit one, looked up at the balcony, at the metallic outlines of a table and chair. He finished his cigarette with his back to the house, leaning against one of the young trees that formed a line between the houses and the field, as if he were a neighbour who'd stepped out for some fresh air. He stubbed out his cigarette on the pavement. Suddenly he felt ridiculous. A pathetic Romeo in his fifties.

Without turning around for fear of seeing her on the balcony, he walked away in the direction of the wasteland.

He entered the fenced-off zone at the far end of the development. It was Saturday night, and there could have been teenagers loitering. They were the only settlers who went in there. Alone, they were harmless. Drunk and in groups, they were uncontrollable mobs.

But that night there were no voices, no laughter, no clinking bottles. The wind was getting colder and must have blown them elsewhere.

24

"He came out of there."

Raquel Gómez was a furious windmill, one arm swinging in the direction of the uninhabited zone, the other towards the body lying on the ground, blocking the entrance to the car park of one of the apartment blocks. The man raised his head a few centimetres to look at the commotion whipping up around him. He was lying in front of a car, lit up by the headlights. A group of about twenty people surrounded the vehicle, keeping their distance because of the man's stench.

She moved a little closer. She could never have imagined a human being could smell that bad. He exuded an overpowering stench of encrusted sweat and dried urine, of rancid dampness and rotting flesh on account of the badly tanned hides he'd fashioned trousers and a waistcoat from. Rabbit skin, cat skin, dog skin, judging by the tails hanging from his belt.

No one dared touch him, although a couple of people were wearing rubber gloves, so they must have made an attempt. The man stared up at them, unresponsive.

"This is too much!"

"Is he drunk?"

"He pissed on the roundabout."

"They stole some plants the other day. And now this."

The circle was widening, growing.

"We should call the police."

Just then, the tramp opened his mouth.

"Oundabout... olice... olice... unk..."

The words came out erratically, interspersed with spasmodic jerks as if he was being electrocuted from the inside.

"No, not the police. What a scandal!"

"Olice... olice... candal..." said the man, then laid his head back on the ground, ready to carry on sleeping despite all the noise.

"And we've got our party this weekend. What will the locals think?"

"It's fucking scandalous! We can't take these squatters any more. Either the police get them out, or we get them out."

Cowardly hands, still protected by rubber gloves, dangled limply by their sides.

At least two phones were already calling the police. The local police. The national police would have to come from the capital and could take over an hour to get there. "They're on their way," said a voice.

A murmur of approval spread through the group. They had gone from victims to guardians. The intruder was not to escape before the officers arrived. It was getting dark.

The police officers would arrive, would heave the body up off the ground; then, after listening to the complaints of the residents, perhaps the homeless man too, they'd put him in the car and take him away. To where?

To the town. And then? In a Western, every tiny one-horse town had a prison. And a sheriff.

A siren could be heard in the distance. She didn't want to see the end of the spectacle. She walked away.

25

He and Matías filled two plastic bottles with water and went to the cemetery.

Sunshine, cicadas, and a cold breeze heralding the autumn. The breeze also brought with it a siren, long before they could see the police car. Out there in the open, there was nowhere to hide. He dropped the bottle and threw himself to the ground. Matías did the same. It was getting closer. He lifted his head. In the distance, the car was gliding rapidly down the main road. The siren was unnecessary as there were no other vehicles around. Perhaps that's why they put it on, like children who sing to themselves when they're home alone.

It whizzed past.

"That's it, keep going to the other side, to the development," said Matías. "Can we get up now?"

They stood up and carried on walking in silence. His heart was racing. He put his free hand in his pocket and gripped the stone tightly. One of its sharp edges dug in and the pain calmed him, although his hands were still shaking as he watered the murdered tramp's plant.

"If you want, tonight we can go to the petrol station and ask the Dominican about it."

The Dominican told them they'd carted off some homeless man who'd showed up on the development.

"I feel more relaxed now," said Matías as they walked back.

"Why?"

"I thought it might have been the junkie."

"Is he still there?"

"Tomorrow I'll go and check. Maybe he's dead. Maybe it was him who appeared to me."

"What do we do if he is?"

"I guess we bury him, son. We're not going to leave him lying about."

He imagined having to dig a grave with a spoon, until he remembered the Dominican had a shovel.

"Poor Teresa!" said the old man. "Not the best company!"

But Teresa and the tramp remained the only two dead bodies there. The following day, Matías confirmed that the drug addict had moved on, to die somewhere else.

In the evening he left the old man at his door and went out into the fields again. He needed to think about what had happened, about the terror he'd experienced when he heard the police siren. It was ridiculous. If his colleagues had tracked him down, they certainly wouldn't make themselves known like that.

He followed the line of houses at a good distance, went through the park, reached the statue of the founder's grandfather and the roundabout. He took out the packet of cigarettes and lit one. He leaned against the edge of the letters, facing the statue. He couldn't deny that he was increasingly enjoying the life he was leading. As important as it was for the others to stop looking for him, he also had to stop thinking about them. He wanted to forget not only what he'd done, but above all the person he was when he did it, and the reasons he'd become so corrupt.

As he smoked, he touched the letters, saying them aloud one by one. He sounded like a child learning to read.

When he finished, as if he had pronounced the magic words, he saw the headlights of a car approaching. Even before it reached him, he knew it was the Mercedes. He hid, like the last time. Like last time, it was midnight and it was Wednesday. And Pacheco repeated his ritual, his penance, his grovelling. A little shorter this time. The nights were starting to get colder. He waited for Pacheco to get all his crying done, get back in the car, and return to his hiding place.

He returned to his.

In the early hours of the morning, the wind got up, blowing freely through the openings where doors and windows should have been. The buildings were suddenly cold.

Cocooned in blankets, he remembered the dark-haired woman in the floral dress kneeling at the edge of the wasteland. The shape of her body under her dress was barely discernible, but it seemed strong, firm. He remembered her smile. Her glasses had prevented him from seeing her eyes. For the first time, he was curious about one of the settlers.

He slept with the blankets pulled right up to his chin. Although he was sweating when he woke in the morning, he had been cold. He couldn't remember if there were any more blankets in Luján's apartment. He'd moved in at a time when the cold was a hypothetical concept.

After washing himself in the bucket of water and drinking a coffee, he went over to the old man's house.

The door was padlocked, the terrace deserted. He found him in the wasteland, emptying a bottle of water over the shrub on his wife's grave. He also tended the other dead man's plant. Seeing him, Matías beckoned to him to come closer.

He looked like he was finding the cold more excruciating. He was rubbing his arms over his clothes even though the sun was warm. He hadn't shaved, and his face looked droopy, baggy. He'd never noticed whether the old man still had his own teeth, or whether they were false.

Matías grumbled a greeting.

"What's the matter?"

"I slept badly."

"They say you sleep less as you get older," he replied. It was a supermarket queue pleasantry because he couldn't think of what to say.

"I didn't say less, I said badly." He paused. Then, looking embarrassed, he confessed quietly, "I kept hearing voices."

"It was the wind, Matías."

"So why were they repeating my name?" He was frightened.

"If you want, I could come and live in your block," he offered, to his own surprise.

The old man smiled at him with the melancholic gratitude of parents when their young children offer to help them sort out their problems: *I'll go and beat up your meanie old boss for you, just you wait and see.*

"It's better the way it is, each of us having our own space. When two people are together in the same place for too long there's always conflict. Take her, for example." He pointed at the ground. "When she got diagnosed, she joined one of those cults that make them stand on street corners handing out pamphlets. Within a week, she was already fighting with her other two companions over who stood on the right, and who stood in the middle. Thank goodness. Saying that, I wouldn't have cared about the cult if it had been a real comfort to her while she was dying. But she was far too rational. As soon as she thought about it properly, she was over it."

He remembered how Matías had told him he was running away from his children, and from a retirement home.

"Don't you miss them?" he'd asked.

"I miss the younger versions of my children. As the men they are now, honestly, not so much."

"Have you not thought about going back to your family?"

"No. Besides, I can't leave her here." Matías shot him a terrified look. "What if it's her?"

"What?"

"The one calling out to me at night. Maybe it's my... turn."

"Come on, let's get out of here."

"It's been days since she last visited me at night."

"That's because you planted that shrub and she's happy."

"No, that's not it. It's because she knows I'll be with her soon and she's waiting for me."

"Stop talking rubbish." He gestured to him to follow. "Let's go."

He started walking. The old man followed him. "That's why I have a favour to ask you."

He started walking faster. He could guess what it was. And no, he didn't want to.

"Normally, when one person says that," said Matías, puffing along behind him, "the other person asks what it is."

"Okay, what is it then? What do you want to ask me?" he said but didn't turn around.

"I want you to bury me next to her when I die."

26

"Fantastic!"

Sergio Morales was ecstatic when the winner of the tortilla-making competition was announced. A local woman who owned the supermarket in town had won it "fair and square". Morales took endless pictures with his phone and urged others to do the same, to document the success. A stream of images of colourful, smiling people ascending to the digital cloud.

The day, Saturday, had showed up in good spirits. The wind had dropped, leaving the air cooler but not so chilly they couldn't wear short sleeves.

She had a creeping suspicion that the others had made an agreement without telling her, because she was the only one wearing a plain blouse among the motley festival of floral prints, orange slices, multicoloured pineapples, exotic birds, branded geometric print motifs, and even a Japanese landscape. They all paraded past, admiring the perfect arrangement of the tables, the decorations, the food, before congratulating Yolanda Vivancos, who received their praise in her pink fern-print blouse.

In the afternoon, wine tasting, a horseshoe-throwing competition, pétanque, a paper-flower workshop for the adults. Hot chocolate, games, and clowns for the children. The settlers' children couldn't understand why their parents kept fervently insisting that they should mingle and play with the local kids. Why wouldn't they? After all, they went to the same school. Their parents, who dropped them off and picked them up every day, seemed to have forgotten that.

At dusk, the twinkling coloured lanterns went on, lighting up the garlands, the autumnal-patterned tablecloths, and the candles in amber glass holders. At one end of the square, a stage. A band with a singer. The middle became the dance floor. The clowns, who'd taken off their make-up, eaten, drunk, and, above all, been paid, had already piled into their van and were on their way back to the capital.

The whole settlement was there. The Wine and Harvest Festival had also attracted many of the locals, "tarted up like they're at a Valencian wedding", as Raquel Gómez put it.

She would have loved to take her walk through the streets right then. It must have looked like one of those towns abandoned shortly before the water is unleashed from a dam, before the houses become underwater ruins, only to reappear when drought rears its ugly cracked head. But she had to be there, at one side of the square, selling tickets from behind the little counter decorated with tissue-paper vine leaves, framed between two young plane trees from which the GRAND TOMBOLA banner hung.

"Don't mention probability to anyone. You IT nerds love explaining that kind of thing," Yolanda Vivancos had told her with a laugh, before entering the fray.

Luckily, she only had another half hour to go. When the band took its break, the raffle would be drawn and then the trophies would be awarded for the finest tortilla de patatas, the best cake, and the pétanque champion.

"I'll take one." It was the woman who worked on reception at the health centre and lived in town.

"Which do you want?"

"The winning one, please," she said, chuckling at her own joke. She handed over a euro. "I haven't seen you at the practice for days."

"That's essentially a good thing, isn't it?"

"Of course, of course," she said, taking the numbered raffle ticket.

On the reverse was a drawing of a bunch of grapes, which had taken countless emails back and forth to agree on. She had systematically ignored all the emails, only to discover later that she'd filed away an epic melodrama, Yolanda Vivancos versus Raquel Gómez, into the recycle bin on her computer. Like the Bette Davis and Joan Crawford feud but over the quantity and layout of a few grapes.

The dance floor was filling up. At the buffet tables it was all carving, chopping, slicing, splitting, stirring, opening, serving... and from time to time, spilling. Hired crockery and cutlery. High-quality plastic that looked like bone china. Metal forks, spoons, and knives. Judging by his sour expression, Ernesto Royo, the treasurer, must have been calculating how many of these items would be returned and how many would end up in the houses of the locals. Morales, on the other hand, could not have been more chuffed with the proceedings. "Eat our food, drink our beer and wine, dance to our music, here, on our soil." The message was also directed at family and friends who'd come from elsewhere: "Look how well we're doing here." From time to time he would kiss his wife on the neck. Natalia, her hair up in a high bun, was startled by the brush of her husband's lips every time, and he laughed happily every time as if making her jump was his intention all along.

Natalia had already noticed the blue felt tip-marked stone she'd made into a pendant necklace. "Make sure it's fastened securely. You know that one's an escapee."

She felt its rough edges brush against her every time she moved, an appreciative graze.

From the puzzled look on Morales's face, she realised he'd recognised his wife's blue mark and was wondering what the pendant meant. But he was the kind of man who preferred not to ask questions when he knew he wasn't going to like the answer.

There were still quite a few tickets left to sell, but it didn't matter; the items that weren't won would be drawn again and again until the winning numbers came up, and the capsule coffee machine, wireless headphones, Japanese kitchen knife set, and numerous house plants with their respective pots all had new owners. There was no probability calculation there. The one-euro tickets were more a way of making it look like they weren't just giving everything away, like the nouveau riche.

It was the time of night when the younger children, overwrought, screamed or cried then fell asleep, absolutely worn out. A tent had been set up for them, a kind of playpen with little beds where three children were already sleeping, guarded by a few old people from the local town who'd brought chairs and a small table to play cards on. Some children were still dancing with their fathers or mothers. There were hardly any teenagers to be seen. Their absence was notable once they'd managed to snaffle some food and bottles of booze. Each generation to its own.

The singer announced the final number before the interval. A bolero, so everyone could wind down for the break. "*Conttiiigo aprrrrendíííí...*" The dance floor was packed.

As the singer and musicians brought the song to a close, in the seconds before the applause there was a scream.

Surrounded by couples dancing cheek to cheek, stood a little boy. He was wearing an enormous Barça shirt that came down to his knees. Bare legs, feet tucked into trainers with the ends cut off and his toes poking out.

"It's one of them!" someone shouted.

The grubby blonde boy raised his hand and crammed a slice of tortilla de patatas into his mouth; then, smiling as he chewed, raised his hand as if to offer them the rest.

"Thief!" cried someone else.

The boy turned in the direction of the shriek. She saw the back of his shirt. Messi, of course. His hand was still in the air, clutching the piece of tortilla, looking for someone to share it with.

Still on stage, the singer coughed nervously into the microphone. That roused Germán, who left the woman he was dancing with, the supermarket owner, who had come first in the tortilla-making competition. He walked up to the boy and whacked the tortilla out of his hand. The remains fell to the ground. The boy stepped forward with a grunt and Germán responded with a slap. The circle closed in, dark, menacing.

She shoved the table aside, scattering the raffle tickets all over the floor. It didn't matter. In that instant she knew there would be no tombola draw, at least not for her.

Forcing her way through the crowd, she squared up to Germán. "Why are you hitting him? He's just a child."

"He's a thief."

"That" – she pointed to the ground – "is a piece of tortilla, a piece of fucking tortilla!"

"He's one of them!" shouted a woman from the throng.

Several people muttered. *Shut up, don't mention them in front of the locals.*

Other people were shouting.

"He's one of them, one of them."

A murmuring around him.

"Thief."

"Police."

"He's one of them."

"What's he doing here?"

The dense, dark wall of bodies, silhouetted by the lights, closed in around him.

Germán looked like he was about to grab the child. She stepped in. "Don't you touch him." She held up her hand to keep him at a distance.

He, blind with rage, raised his fist.

A voice halted him: "Stop!" It was Morales.

"What do you want?" Germán said, confronting him. Fist clenched, but down by his side.

"Stop it."

"Can't you see what's happening? They're sneaking in." He looked around, searching for other intruders.

Others imitated him, and this made him bolder.

"Do you think this one's alone? I'm sure there are more hiding out there, waiting to rob us."

She rested a hand on the boy's shoulder. It felt like touching the bones of a bird.

More suspicious, frightened glances around, while Germán took a breath, raised his index finger, and pointed at her.

"And then *she* goes and defends them. Why don't you just invite them?" He turned to Morales now. "Yeah, why don't you organise another little party and invite them too? I'm sick to death of all you bloody do-gooders!"

She drew the child towards her. She took his soft little hand, greasy with bits of eggy potato.

The crowd was closing in further. Even though they were outdoors, in a square, there seemed to be hardly any air. Something dark that oozed from their pores had tainted their clothes. There were no more flowers, palm trees, or pineapples in the prints; the polo jockeys, crocodiles, and American university logos had also vanished from the men's T-shirts. Everything was black.

As the boy squeezed her hand, she looked up at the crowd's faces. Two shades of anger: the pale white of pressed lips, and vociferous red. They had to get out of there. She started walking, pulling the child with her.

Germán grabbed her arm. "Where do you think you're going?"

"I'm taking him back to his family."

She tugged herself out of his grip with a sudden movement. When he tried to grab her again, Germán ripped the necklace with the stone pendant from around her neck. It fell to the ground.

"Leave her alone!" Morales ordered.

All of Germán's aggression was immediately focused on Morales. She took the opportunity to break out of the circle, pushing people aside with her free hand.

She was almost out when a body stood in her way: the gardener, arms crossed, legs apart, was blocking her path. He was about to say something when someone pulled him by his waistband and moved him aside.

"Hey, what are you doing?"

"Get out of the way!" It was his wife.

She left the mob behind and reached the foot of the stage, where the musicians still stood, motionless, as if waiting to be told what the soundtrack should be for the action below. She rounded the stage and found a side street. "Run," she said.

With the boy holding her hand and following obediently, they swiftly left the streets of the development behind. Phase 1. Phase 2. Phase 3. They reached Phase 4. There, total darkness. She'd never done the route leading to the end of the constructions at night before.

Nobody followed them.

She stopped and asked the boy, "Where do you live?"

Before he could answer, she was startled by a noise coming from behind the boundary fence. Something was moving between the buildings. The boy squeezed her hand to reassure her.

"There you are!" A man's voice.

The shadow came closer and stayed on the other side of the fence. It was the man with the grey hair.

"His parents are looking for him. Where was he?"

"You could say he crashed a party. How do I get him through?" She looked for an opening in the fence.

"There." He motioned her forward and walked along with her on the other side of the fence. He moved confidently in spite of the lack of light. He had the slightly ambling gait of long-legged men. The child wouldn't let go of her hand.

"What's your name?" she asked the boy.

The boy squeezed her hand again, twice. Two syllables?

"Don't you want to tell me?"

"He doesn't usually talk," said the man.

"What's his name?"

"I don't know, to be honest."

"In that case, we'll call you Boy."

The man laughed. So did the boy: a deep, throaty laugh.

"Like Boy in the Tarzan films."

The man stopped and pushed at a section of the wire to open a hole in the fence. She'd always feared something similar might happen during her walks, and couldn't help but recoil slightly. She let go of the boy's hand, and he slipped through to the other side.

"Bye, Boy."

The boy looked at her and waved. It was too dark to see, but his hand must have been shiny with oil like hers. "Messi," he said. Like his laugh, his voice was faltering, hoarse.

"Bye, Messi."

The boy started heading off into the darkness.

"I'd better go, before he gets lost again," said the man, and thanked her. He was already walking away when he turned and asked, "Wouldn't you like to meet his parents? They'll be very grateful to you."

All she could see of the boy now was the faint white number ten on his back.

"Couldn't we do it in the daytime?"

"Would you come then?"

They agreed to meet the following morning.

As she got closer to the inhabited zone and the lights, the music started up again. It sounded slightly distorted from where she was. Morales had managed to keep the party going. Not for her.

She took a detour home. She washed the grease off her hands. There was a mark on the back of her neck, a dark red line where the necklace with the stone pendant had been. She poured herself a Campari, which she swallowed in one gulp, on the balcony, to wash down the pill. The wind was getting up again, stirring the leaves of the eleven poplars and shaking the treetops of the phantom forest in the distance.

She could still hear the music and all the racket from her bedroom, so she closed the windows.

27

The wind had blown confetti into the first streets of the uninhabited zone, rustling swirls of shredded paper with grubby little faces. In spite of its noble purpose, paper is always competing with food scraps, scrabbling for first place in the race to become rubbish. Crumpled sheets of damp newspaper in a showdown with orange peel.

They'd agreed to meet early in the morning at the end of the tarmac road. He waited for her behind the wall where he'd been when he first saw her, so he wouldn't be exposed and she wouldn't feel watched as she approached. Although he couldn't help peering over it a few times.

She arrived right on time. Even though it was cool, she was wearing the flowery dress she'd worn the first time he saw her. Was it a hint? That was a mystery better left unsolved, because it would lose its meaning whether the conjecture turned out to be right or wrong.

They greeted each other shyly, not quite sure what to do

with their hands, following an absurdly formal handshake. He missed not having something to give her. It was then he understood the significance of a bouquet of flowers, but at the foot of the fence there were only nettles and small plants with wild-looking stems. With a sweeping gesture of his arm, he invited her into the zone.

"Is the boy okay?" she asked.

It took him a while to answer. It was the first time he'd seen her up close and could make out the details of her face, the big brown eyes behind her glasses, the slightly crooked smile.

"Yes. He was just a bit scared, although in his own way. I think he has some form of autism."

She didn't ask him any more questions. She looked at the streets and buildings with the curiosity of an explorer.

"You've never been here before?"

"No. I've always been a bit scared of it."

"Why? They're only empty apartments."

"Not all of them. You live here."

"Do I look dangerous to you?" He instantly felt childish; no, more than that, he felt stupid.

Before he could say anything to make a better impression, she stopped and grabbed his arm. She'd seen Matías; he was sitting on the front steps of the building where the family lived.

"He's a friend," he told her, even if that was currently a lie.

Matías came over and gave him a resentful look. Although they'd both helped out in the search the previous night, they hadn't spoken to each other since he'd refused the old man's request to bury him alongside his wife. Matías smiled at her. He was fiddling with the little doll that had been the victim of the boy's tower demolition.

"Are you the one who found the boy?" He stood up, shook her hand, and offered her the raggedy one-armed doll. "A thank-you gift."

She took it, looked at it tenderly, and slipped it into one of the pockets of her dress.

"They left as soon as the sun came up. It's a pity you didn't get to meet them," said Matías. "They were so grateful to you. Coffee?"

"Sure."

"Okay, come with me." Matías took the woman's arm, then turned to him and said, "You too, if you like."

He assumed that she didn't realise what was going on and that, if she sensed the old man's animosity towards him, she didn't seem to care.

They climbed the stairs without a handrail in single file. The old man in front, her next, without the vertigo that made him stay glued to the wall behind them, avoiding looking into the stairwell. He focused on the woman's strong calves in front of him, which led him step by step up to Matías's apartment. She took it all in with unabashed curiosity.

Matías led them into the living room and disappeared into his room to make the coffee. He stood leaning against a wall with his hands in his trouser pockets. In his right pocket he turned the blue-marked stone over and over, while she, without reacting or saying anything, observed the old man's place: the piles of books, the chairs, the plastic sheets covering the balcony and the windows.

"Do you live like this too?" she asked.

"Yep, but in another apartment."

"Of course. There are plenty of them."

Now, logically, should come the question about why he was there; however, the woman went over to the window and looked out at the buildings and streets.

The naturalness with which she then sat down on one of the rickety chairs to have coffee with them, the way she made light, easy conversation with the old man, and above all, the fact that she didn't ask them any questions, far from being pleasant or reassuring, offended him. It was as if she wasn't taking them seriously, as if this encounter was simply material for an amusing anecdote, something to tell her friends back in the settlement.

Oblivious to his suspicions, Matías was holding forth on the coexistence of humans and animals. He was getting to the part where he defended the rights of the animals already living there when the apartments were built, bolstering his argument with a list of species.

"You're very knowledgeable," she commented.

"Nonsense. Most knowledge is acquired to stave off boredom."

"If that's the case, I take it back. Actually, I only said what I thought you wanted to hear. Just being polite really."

She gave a sly chuckle at the surprised look on the face of the old man, who laughed too in the end, although it took him a while. Then they talked about the boy and his family.

"Do you know where they went?"

"To the coast," he replied.

"Towards Alicante, I think," added Matías.

"That's a long way," she said.

"They have a van," said the old man.

"It's the same distance in a van," she said.

Again, the look of confusion on Matías's face. "I don't suppose you've got many friends," he replied, slightly disgruntled.

He stifled a laugh.

"You neither." She smiled and finished her coffee. "Are there many of you here?"

"Why do you want to know?" Matías asked.

"Just curious. Why are you worried about me asking you? Are you afraid of something?"

"Is there something I should be afraid of?"

"No." She stood up somewhat abruptly. "Well, I'd better get going."

Like a polite and courteous guest, she thanked them for the coffee, gave what he thought was a slight bow, and left. It all happened so fast that they were still sitting there as her footsteps echoed down the stairs.

Matías took a deep breath.

"If you make any Cinderella jokes, I'll throw you off the balcony and bury you, but next to the tramp," he said before the old man could open his mouth.

"So you'll do it? You'll bury me when I die?" The old man stood up and hugged him.

"You're such a git, Matías."

28

Out in the street, she looked up at the window holes, behind which were the old man and the other man. How had they ended up there? Who were they? She'd watched them, searching in vain for some gesture, some movement that might reveal what they'd done before, because if they wouldn't tell her, she wasn't going to ask. To do so would be to judge, to invalidate who they were now, whether they had chosen this or it had been thrust upon them.

How many more people were hiding out in those apartments? The rumours doing the rounds among the settlers ranged from those who said they were a bunch of homeless people passing through, to those who imagined hordes of social outcasts preparing to invade. The border lines were not as clearly drawn as the fence made it seem, either. There was a rumour that a young couple, who some claimed to have seen in the mini mart, had started out as squatters in the Phase 2 apartment they lived in, but nobody could go round there and demand to see their paperwork.

Anyway, she couldn't work out whether they were real people or yet another fantasy. Like the urban legend of the girl at the bend in the road, they had the clandestine couple in Phase 2.

They were 236 in number. The council carried out the residents' census like they were an endangered species, although not one in serious danger of extinction. This is declared when only fifty specimens of a species remain. But their offspring would leave when they grew up. Depopulation would happen, just as it did in rural areas. Residential developments full of old people, visited by their children and grandchildren at weekends and on national holidays; paella, indigestion, dozing. Then goodbye. After visiting their parents in prison, the children left. Sometimes the parents went out on temporary release. But never for long; nowhere quite beats a prison of one's own choosing.

She was lost. She couldn't remember seeing that cement mixer on the way there. She stopped looking up at the windows, afraid she'd find someone watching her. On one of the walls was a poster for the development's opening party, now a distant memory. The poster had not been taken down because it was sealed off in the zone. A beetle with a glossy sheen wandered across the faded face of the singer. For a second it became a chitinous moustache with dark-red highlights, before settling in the half-open mouth.

Finally, she reached the fence. A sudden cage-like sensation. She walked along it, looking for the gap from the night before, but she had no reference points for whether to walk to the right or to the left. She went to the right because it brought her closer to the development, and eventually she found a hole, round like a cannonball. She hadn't noticed it before on her walks, perhaps because it was half hidden among some tall grass. She came out on the other side, careful not to lose her little passenger: the doll peeking out of her pocket. Her right leg brushed against a bank of stinging nettles growing just inside the fence. An instant burning sensation. She swore out loud. She would have pulled them up or kicked them, but taking revenge on a nettle is impossible while wearing a summer dress and without gloves. Had she been stung for going in there, or because she was leaving?

Eyes watering from the pain, fighting the urge to itch, she limped slightly as she walked away.

"Is there something to be afraid of?" Matías had asked. She hoped not, but she couldn't forget the faces of the people at the party either. And now the boy's family had left, or rather they appeared to have fled. To the coast. To the sea. So far.

She reached the development. The remnants of the party were still there. How could they have not cleared up yet?

It was Sunday. Very early in the morning.

Only the garlands kept their composure despite the wind which had blown so many lanterns to the ground, where they mingled with paper, bottles, and leftover food. In the air, a sickly-sweet smell, the slow evaporation of all the spilled liquids. The wind had emptied the ashtrays, except the ones where cigarette butts floated in the dregs of cocktails. A group of rodents, maybe voles, were having a feast on one of the tables. "Eat our food, drink our beer and wine, dance to our music, here, on our soil." But there was no music now. The band, like the clowns, had already gone back to the capital.

She left the voles to enjoy their party before the gardener appeared with his decapitating spade.

As she rounded a corner, she saw Raquel Gómez coming out into the street with a broom and a roll of bin bags. She waved as she drew closer. Raquel gave herself a theatrical slap on the forehead as if she'd remembered something, and doubled back into her garden. As she passed their villa, she thought she noticed the Roman blinds on the ground floor twitch surreptitiously. Nobody had net curtains on the development.

Although she didn't see anyone else on her way home, that trivial incident worried her. Could she have been spotted leaving that morning, heading for the uninhabited apartment blocks? Why should she be worried about something like that? Because in that small gesture, the exaggerated display Raquel had put on to avoid her, there was a message: she was contaminated. She'd touched one of the others. She'd taken him away. Perhaps they also knew she'd been going into the uninhabited zone.

She was spiralling into absurd, paranoid conjecture. She made herself look around her, at her shelves full of books, her notebooks, pens, computers... You're at home. Come back from the darkness.

Out of the pocket of her dress she took the one-armed doll. Its right arm was missing. She declared it left-handed. It might have been a character from a cartoon series, because although its proportions were natural the eyes were disproportionately large. She took the doll into the kitchen and washed it under running water before leaving it sitting on her desk, leaning against the foot of the lamp.

Powering up her computer, she reviewed what she'd programmed over the past few days. According to Matías, the bugs on the development had to be respected, but she was free to eliminate all the bugs she caught in the program. "I don't suppose you've got many friends," he'd also said. No, she didn't, and on top of that she made stereotypical IT nerd jokes.

She worked all morning, taking short breaks to go out into her little garden, where she could hear the distant voices of children, the sound of a car, dogs barking. After her lunch break, silence descended: the silence of a Sunday afternoon on the development. Only the song of the cicadas and the rustle of the leaves of the eleven poplars came through the tilted window of her studio. Suddenly, footsteps. Over there? She went over to the window. The little conjoined-twin couple from the white villa were walking arm in arm along the pavement flanked by the saplings.

From the nonchalant way they moved, gesturing with their hands towards the empty horizon, and, above all, the obvious effort they were making not to glance in the direction of her house, she realised that was precisely why they were there. This place was the end of the development, equivalent to the end of civilisation. Past those poplars, there was only barbarism in the form of a hostile wilderness. Nobody ever passed through that part of the development, which wasn't beautiful, even in spring, and even less so now as autumn was finishing off what the summer hadn't managed to consume. The only attraction had to be her. She was being talked about, and these two hadn't been able to contain their curiosity.

Okay then. Wanna see me? She banged on the glass. They both spun round, letting go of each other's arm. She waved at them. They returned her wave, visibly alarmed, then moved out of sight.

She turned off the computer and left the house. She crossed the development at a brisk pace, zigzagging through the streets. She nodded to the few people she passed, not pausing to see if they nodded back.

Wanna see me? Well, here I am.

She crossed the square, where the gardener was sweeping up the last traces of the party. Only the bare stage was still standing, waiting to be dismantled. There were no tables, no chairs, no posters, no raffle tickets, no certificates for the winners of the competitions, no ashtrays, no drinks cans, no leftover food. She hoped the voles had had enough time to fill their bellies before fleeing back to their burrows. The gardener must have seen her go past, but he pretended that the broom and his role as street-sweeper required all his attention.

Morales drove past, and she waved to him. She also waved at the statue of Pacheco's grandfather. She waved at the letters on the roundabout as she went around them. A lizard created an acute accent on the O of Pacheco. Sensing her presence, it swiftly vanished.

She went home.

There, when she turned on her computer, she found a message from Morales calling an extraordinary meeting of the residents' association that night to "take stock of the party". The apparent neutrality of this phrasing, which skirted around the issue of the boy, was the most disturbing thing about it. But she had to go. Her absence would have been seen as a confession of guilt, whatever it was she was guilty of.

She felt cold when she came in, and not because lately the temperature dropped as soon as the sun went down. Pretending not to notice the indifference she was met with, she sat down on her usual sofa, computer on lap. On the table, some drinks and a few bowls of nuts.

"We're all still recovering from yesterday's excesses," said Morales, with a booming baritone laugh that made him sound like Father Christmas.

As the others took their seats, she wrote down the names of everyone in attendance. "Is there an agenda?" she asked.

"That's what it said in the email," replied Ernesto Royo reproachfully.

She crossed out the word "treasurer", which she'd written after his name, and replaced it with "total moron". She felt the burn of the nettles on her right ankle.

"I saw that, but it doesn't hurt to double-check, does it?"

Royo huffed and glanced around, seeking support for – she had to admit – her fairly rude tone.

Morales immediately jumped in: "Right, let's start with the pros."

She found herself writing a summary of the party which, however much she might rework it later at home, had the feel of a primary school essay along the lines of: "my last holiday", "what I did this Christmas", or "a weekend with my parents at Disneyland Paris". The meeting's attendees went through the list of planned activities and their results in a detached manner, as though they were filling out a form, because they were gearing up for what would be point two on the agenda:

"Right. Now we have no choice but to move on to the cons."

She looked up, raised her fingers from the keyboard, and waited like a concert soloist for the conductor's signal, even though she knew she would be one of the themes on the score. The movement began calmly, in an almost objective tone, when Morales referred to the child's appearance at the party. But this calm inevitably only lasted a few seconds, given the seething presence of Germán, who was yet to say a word.

"So you think it's normal for these people to sneak into our party and steal from us?"

He didn't look at her as he spoke, and she wasn't about to repeat what he'd said at the time, which everyone there had heard.

"We cannot stand by and do nothing yet again. Who knows how many more of them were infiltrating the crowd, eating and drinking at our expense, posing as locals. With everything they've stolen, they'll have enough to get them through the winter."

"Don't exaggerate, Germán," said Natalia.

"How do you know I'm exaggerating? You don't even know how many of them there are. Whole cases of beer, wine, and soft drinks went missing. Not to mention the food."

She bit her lip. What she wanted to say, and didn't, was that it had probably been swiped by their own little darlings. She balanced the laptop on the arm of the sofa so she could rub her right leg gently, trying not to scratch it.

Suddenly Germán challenged her: "Why aren't you writing down what I'm saying? Don't you think it's important?"

"In the minutes I record data, proposals, and resolutions. I don't write down speculation or accusations."

"And who are you to decide what's what?"

"It's my role. That's why you chose me."

Morales quickly intervened: "That's right."

There was no time for a reply from Germán. Sitting opposite her, Yolanda Vivancos uncrossed the arms with which she seemed to have been restraining herself this entire time.

"What did you do with the boy?"

"What would you like me to have done with him, Yolanda?" She could have given a more diplomatic or conciliatory answer, but the accusatory tone of the question had prevented her.

Raquel did it for her: "Don't have a go at Yolanda, she put so much effort into organising the party so we could make friends with the locals... And then that child came along and almost ruined everything."

"Well, the party went on."

"But I'm sure the locals are all talking now," said the male half of the conjoined-twin couple.

"And what do you think they'd be saying if something had happened to that child?" Common sense stopped her from using the word "lynch".

"Where did you take him?" This time it was Natalia asking. She did give her a reply.

"To the blocks of empty apartments, where I imagined his parents must be. But the main thing is that I took him away from here, from all of you, but especially from you." She pointed at Germán. "You went ballistic over an omelette. Was it so terrible, what the kid did? Or was it because he took a piece of the winning tortilla?" Her voice was so heavily laced with sarcasm that she barely recognised it.

Morales stood up so he could look down on them. "Let's all just calm down a bit."

"If you say so," said Germán, attempting to tone down the aggression. "We'll talk as calmly as you like, but we can't let the situation go on like this. We have to do something about these people before they do something to us."

They all agreed with him in one way or another, all the while looking at her, waiting for her to reply. Even Morales was now on Germán's side. The gardener, buoyed by the general consensus, looked at her with a disdainful pout. He hadn't forgiven her for the shove and public telling-off he'd got from his wife. Natalia, the only one who didn't show any animosity towards the squatters, had disappeared off into the kitchen. She was on her own.

On her own against those in favour of calling the police; on her own against those who didn't want to do that but wanted to solve the problem themselves. Her interventions were ignored; when she spoke, some of them blatantly took the opportunity to pour themselves a drink or grab a handful of nuts, not even looking at her. Then the dispute between the two factions carried on, a discussion of which there would be no record.

"This meeting isn't official," Morales decided. "Delete the notes."

"This is just an informal meeting," added Royo, the lawyer. He got up and stood behind her to make sure she deleted the document. She didn't know whether he'd read what she'd written after his name, but he certainly must have seen the red mark on the back of her neck.

After closing her computer, she stood up. "I can see I'm not needed here, so I'm going."

Other than a half-hearted attempt from Morales, nobody did anything to stop her. She left.

Natalia was outside smoking a cigarette, leaning casually against the door of the garage full of stones. She said goodbye, without asking why she was leaving the meeting.

She didn't feel like going home yet. After that meeting she knew she was in for a night of insomnia, or the alternative, the red slumber induced by pills and Campari.

Although there were watchful eyes spying on her, she left the well-lit area and walked in the direction of the blocks of empty apartments.

She followed the tarmac road in the dark, found the gap in the fence, and slipped through it.

She hadn't a clue where he lived and couldn't remember how to get to Matías's apartment either, seeing as last time she had got lost and taken a detour. Plus this time it was night. She illuminated the uneven ground with her phone torch and prayed to the goddess of coincidence. She did not recognise anything, although she came across the hungry cement mixer again. It occurred to her, too late, that she should mark her route somehow so she could retrace it on the way back. But, on second thoughts, she wasn't exactly entering a labyrinth. It was a simple grid designed by the developer's architects. Using a set square. "Every few streets, pop a little square in for me, so you get to use that semicircle ruler thingy too," Pacheco would have told them. He meant the semicircular protractor children were always made to buy, on the back-to-school list passed down from generation to generation, and which never got used because not even the teachers knew what it was for.

A rustle in the distance. She forced herself to keep concentrating on the ground, to resist the urge to shine her torch at the entrances to the blocks. Flashback to poorly resolved childhood terrors, the fear of opening a door and discovering a monster behind it. Her imagination was ready to take over, but she managed to stop it the same way she warded off fear when she was little: with the game.

Just one more street, let's see if you can hold on one more street. Good! Victory! Now two more. Let's go for it. If I play against myself and lose, have I really lost? Come on, two more streets, there's a brave girl.

She'd almost succeeded, had overcome the ridiculous challenge she'd set for herself, when she heard a whistling sound and stopped dead in her tracks. She held up her phone and shone the light left and right. She heard the whistle again and spun round in a circle, illuminating all around herself. Nothing.

A familiar voice made her look up. "Hey. Here. Up here. Hang on. I'll come down," he said, as naturally as a little boy coming out to play.

The grey-haired man appeared with a torch.

"What are you doing here?"

"I've had a bad day. Don't ask me any more about it."

The man stood next to her, switched off his torch, stuffed his hand in his pocket, and held out the crook of his arm to her. "You don't need a phone. I know these streets."

She linked his arm through his and they started walking, keeping pace with one another. She stumbled over something, a stone or a piece of brick, and moved closer to him. "Where's Matías?" she asked.

"He's usually asleep by now."

Once her eyes had adjusted to the darkness she could make out the outlines of the buildings. They came to the opposite side of the tarmac road she occasionally walked along. To the right, she recognised a low cube intended to be a cultural centre with a library. She had gazed at it glumly in the promotional brochures for the development, which she'd kept. The fact that the development planned to have a library, even a tiny one, had helped her ex-husband to dispel some of her misgivings.

She wanted to go and have a look at the cube, but he stopped her.

"Let's go over there instead, so I can show you another point where you can get in."

A gaping hole in the fence allowed them out into the surrounding fields, the same piece of open land, in fact, that her house looked out over.

They walked along in total darkness, the man guiding her as if she were a blind person. They circled the perimeter fence, away from the buildings and, she noticed underfoot, reached the main road.

"It'll be easier for you along here."

She didn't let go of his arm, however. They walked along in silence as far as the official entrance to the development, the roundabout emblazoned with the name of the developer, and the entrance to the park where the statue of Pacheco's grandfather stood. The development's own Pillars of Hercules, the end of the known world. Beyond, dragons and sea monsters. Lizards and voles.

"I come here most nights to sit and smoke," he said.

In the dark, she grinned mischievously. So it was him leaving the cigarette butts that made the gardener furious. She didn't mention it; she didn't want to talk about those people.

"I'll walk you home."

"It might be dangerous if they see you."

"I don't care."

29

"It might be dangerous if they see you."

"I don't care."

It was true. He was also on the verge of telling her all about Pacheco's Wednesday appearances, the weeping, the penance. But he didn't know this woman, he didn't know what she was doing there or what she wanted, or why she had come to find him.

They trudged along the ghostly avenue with its headless lamp posts and spaces intended for benches, which had turned into beds of weeds instead. They reached the first inhabited houses and the first intact street lamps. Walking at night on road that had tarmac, paving slabs, and, most of all, street lamps had become something unusual for him. The excessive light hurt his eyes. The strangest thing, however, was feeling the warmth of a body. A body to which he was adjusting his pace.

He was not the only one to be dazzled. A scorched moth landed on the pavement at their feet. "How many insects do you reckon are burned to death every night by street lamps?" he asked.

"According to the statistics, it's about a hundred and fifty per lamp post," she replied. She said it decisively, as if she'd been waiting for him to ask this ludicrous question.

They went along counting lamp posts and multiplying them by the number of dead insects. A few days later, he would remember that as the exact moment he started falling in love with her.

He left her at her front door.

"See you again?" she asked, still holding on to his arm.

"Any time. But you'd better come in the daytime, so you can say hello to Matías too. He'll be pleased to see you."

He didn't want to tell her that, a couple of days ago, three dangerous-looking men had broken into the building intended for the library. They'd had an enormous brown dog with them. Matías was wary, although the Dominican at the petrol station had told him the dog must be well fed because they'd bought his entire stock of dog food. One of the men had looked ill or injured. He didn't want to find out. Surely the men would move along soon anyway.

She pulled away from him, opened the garden gate, and went into the house.

His side felt cold all the way back. That night he took out one of the blankets he was using as a mattress, and covered himself with it.

*

They met again two days later, in the afternoon. The somewhat old-fashioned man inside him felt the need to show her something during the walk, but there was little to show other than crumbling buildings, rubble, scraggly weeds, and rubbish. So he took her to the building where Matías said there were ghosts.

It didn't look any different to the adjacent buildings. A few ground-floor apartments open to the elements, exposed brickwork, loose cables waiting for a new gang of plunderers, chipped concrete columns, the smell of damp, rusted metal, and dust. The light of that cold, blue-sky day turned to grey inside, the gloom making them more sombre too. It darkened her skin, drained the colour from her turquoise jumper.

They sat on some planks. The suspended dust particles floated softly, trying not to touch the ground, before they were stirred up again by a blast of air. He felt the cold breeze on the back of his neck and pulled up the collar of his jacket. Then, he told her the story of the two labourers who'd died while working there, and joked about Matías's fear that their ghosts roamed the building.

"What would they be like, the ghosts that haunt houses that never ended up being lived in?" she wondered. "They must feel uncomfortable, a bit displaced, because they never thought they'd end up dying here."

Afraid of offending her, he hardly dared to ask her the question: "Do you believe in—"

"No. Ghosts don't exist. But perhaps these two don't know that."

An ill-timed reflection in the lenses of her glasses shielded her eyes from him, so he couldn't tell if she was pulling his leg. He kept quiet about it, along with all the other unknowns he chose not to ask her about.

It was getting late. The light was barely trickling in. "Shall we go?" he said. He was cold in spite of his jacket and could feel sadness rising in his throat.

"Wait. We have to do a good deed." She found the stairwell to the non-existent stairs, looked up, and, cupping her hands round her mouth, shouted, "Hey! You two. Just to let you know, ghosts don't exist!" She looked at him. "Don't suppose you know their names, do you?"

"Why would I know?"

She shrugged and looked up again. "Paco, Pepe, Antonio, Juan, Rafael, Manuel, Jesús, Sergio, Mateo, David. Ghosts don't exist. Marcelo, Julio, Óscar, Federico, Fernando, Pablo, Pedro, Aníbal, Saturnino. Ghosts don't exist."

"Aníbal? Saturnino? Really?"

"Just in case."

"You know you're a weirdo, right?" He offered her his arm again.

"Yep, afraid so." She stood next to him.

That warmth was nice. He kissed her on the top of the head, although she didn't seem to notice.

"Come on. Matías is waiting for us."

They'd taken a couple of steps when he stopped. There was something he needed to do. He dragged her back to the spot where she'd shouted out the names, looked up into the blackness of the building and shouted, "And you can tell Matías ghosts don't exist!"

30

Distracted, her mind wandered to Matías's rooftop, three days ago, where she'd surreptitiously observed the man's profile. She liked his nose, large and beautifully curved.

She remembered the soft touch of his lips on her head.

She imagined suggesting that they visit the building again, to shout out more names and set the ghosts of the dead labourers free.

She kept replaying their last goodbye over and over in her mind; it was futile, like trying to edit a film's ending to make it better.

"When will we see each other again?" he had asked.

"I don't know. I've got a lot of work on."

"I understand."

It was impossible to erase the tone of disappointment in that "I understand", which meant he couldn't have possibly understood, the same way he couldn't know what she was concealing behind that feeble excuse. He couldn't know that '"a lot of work" meant she needed to cling to routine to survive. Without it she would become soft like a shell-less tortoise. Without it she would be exposed to the elements, she would dry out, crack, and die, dehydrated and desiccated. Then she'd be eaten by ants.

So she'd said she had a lot of work to do, he'd replied that he understood, and they'd said goodbye.

When will we see each other again? I don't know. I've got a lot of work on. I understand.

She was stuck in an endless, painful loop. His face as he said, "I understand" and left her at her front door.

No, you don't understand. You can't understand, she thought as she shut the door. And she went out again to call after him, to ask him to stay, but he'd already disappeared. She went round the back. Only the eleven poplars were there.

The burn of the stinging nettles brought her back to the present. She went down to the kitchen and rubbed an ice cube where it hurt.

That night she went to bed without taking any pills.

At around three in the morning she was woken by something clattering against the bedroom window. She was worried a bird had flown into the glass. That had happened once before. She'd spent an hour crying helplessly beside the dying bird, which was wrapped in a towel she later used as its shroud.

She got out of bed when she heard another small *bonk* on the window.

Pebbles.

Being thrown by Natalia, from the garden fence. She looked out over the balcony. Natalia was gesticulating at her.

"Come."

"Where to?"

"I need your help."

"With what?"

"Don't ask questions. Come down." Her voice was imperious.

She got dressed and joined her outside.

Natalia was wearing sportswear under her leather jacket. But she'd done her make-up as if she was going on a night out, and was wearing sparkly earrings.

"What do you want?"

"You'll see in a minute."

She accompanied Natalia to her house. Or rather she followed her, because Natalia set off without waiting for a response. She walked with her body upright and her arms rigid, paddling through the air as if wading through dense matter. At that hour, the streets were deserted. The brightness of the street lamps made them even emptier; there were no dark corners where imaginary monsters might lurk.

They got to the villa. Natalia opened the door to the garage where she stored the crates full of stones. "Let's set them free," she said, turning to face her for the first time. She talked in a whisper but was clearly excited.

"What?"

"We're going to get them out of here. I can't bear them being locked up."

"You and me?"

"See anyone else around here?"

She tried to protest, but Natalia stepped forward. "Please. Just trust me."

"How are we supposed to carry all of this?"

"In my husband's car."

Five minutes later they were loading the crates of stones into Morales's pickup. Natalia had planned everything thoroughly. She'd spread a blanket over the back part of the truck so the crates wouldn't make a sound.

"So what now?" she asked as they finished. She'd worked up a sweat. "Where do you want us to leave them?"

"Here and there."

At that time of night, it all seemed fine to her. Somewhere between amused and scared, between a helper and a henchman, she listened to the final instructions: she was to drive slowly through the streets of the development so Natalia, who would be lying on her front in the cargo bed with the tailgate open, could drop the stones without making too much noise.

So that's what they did, leaving a trail of stones in their wake, like Ariadne's thread through the labyrinth that none of them could apparently escape from. The image of Sergio Morales as a pot-bellied Minotaur replaced that bleak thought and made her smile.

"What's so funny?" Natalia had sat up to get another load of stones and glimpsed her in the rear-view mirror.

"We're like Hansel and Gretel," she replied. She didn't want to offend her by sharing the mental image of her husband.

Nobody would eat those crumbs. We all know what happened to the wolf after they filled his belly with stones.

Two more streets and they were done. She parked the car in front of the villa. The garage door was still open. Suddenly, a light went on inside the house.

"He's awake. You'd better go. Don't let him see you with me."

Natalia gave her a big hug, which felt like a farewell.

On her way home she wished that for once the street lamps would go out and the pebbles could shine in the moonlight to show her the way.

She flopped into bed. The exhaustion brought with it a sudden flash of clarity: the Grimms' story is inconsistent. If the parents abandon Hansel and Gretel in the forest because they don't have anything to feed them with, where does the boy get all the bread he marks the path with the first time? It was a single flash, as the consequences of what they'd just done didn't cross her mind.

31

An illusion. He was shackling himself to an illusion.

From the roof of his building, he looked towards the development, where, hidden behind the apartment blocks, there was her terraced house. He was reminded of a pain he thought he'd managed to shut out, a bittersweet melancholy as he remembered their goodbye. Like a shy teenager being rejected by the girl. The weird girl, too. The short-sighted, strong-legged woman with a head full of quirky facts, which she reeled out to make him laugh. How could he miss her so much when he hardly knew her?

This was what happened when he let emotions into his life. As if he didn't have enough with Matías.

Matías and his obsession with being buried next to his wife. He'd made friends with an old dog, and not only do you have to keep an old dog company, and groom it, you also have to bury it, because it goes and dies on you.

He should have stood his ground that day when Matías had asked him.

*

"I want you to bury me next to her when I die."

He had walked off at a considerable pace to get away from Matías, from the grave that bound him to that place. But the old man had followed him.

"Promise me you will!"

He went on like this until they reached the first buildings.

"Promise me! It's no big deal."

No big deal? It was a huge deal.

"What makes you think I'll even be here when you die?" he'd yelled.

"But I promised her."

Nothing is as binding as promises made to the dead; it was cruel to deny Matías that promise, but the part of him that had always been cruel spoke up.

"That's not my problem."

Then there was the lost boy, the search, her holding the child's hand. Messi smelling of tortilla de patatas.

The next day, her again, and Matías extracting a promise that he would bury him next to his wife.

Perhaps he'd missed a great opportunity. Forced isolation from other human beings had opened the door to absolute freedom, without any ties, emotions, or attachments. He relinquished that freedom every time he worried about that daft old codger or was glad to see him. He was relinquishing it as he shivered on the rooftop, looking out towards the edge of the development where she lived.

He stood up and looked out over the surrounding fields. Far away, perhaps not far enough, they were still looking for him. He must not forget that.

32

Without doxylamine or one of its merciful sisters acting as guardians of sleep, the vibration of a phone can shatter it in an instant. Morales. He wanted to see her urgently round at his house. She already knew what this was about. Another "informal" neighbourhood meeting, to discuss the stones. A bit of a prank, that's all it had been. She hoped the others would see it that way. Or most of them at least.

Out in the street, she was astonished to find that the stones had vanished. Though she walked all the way with her head down, she didn't see a single one. But she didn't need crumbs or pebbles to find her way to the villa.

She rang the doorbell at the garden gate, which immediately swung open. They were expecting her. In the hallway, she discovered that she should have phrased that sentence in the singular: just Sergio Morales. Sergio Morales, and the overpowering scent of vanilla in the house.

"Where's Natalia?"

"She's gone to the capital for a few days. As you're fully aware, she wasn't very well."

Morales closed the door to the street but did not open the door leading into the house. For what he was about to say, the hallway was apparently sufficient.

"What happened last night... I don't even know what to call it," he began.

The serious look on his face and the absence of Natalia had robbed her of words as well.

"It's not right what you did, it's not normal."

"Didn't you know your wife was keeping all those stones in the garage?"

"Natalia had her strange habits, but they were harmless and, most of all, discreet. Yesterday, though, everyone saw it."

He thought she was the ringleader. And she wasn't going to contradict him. She couldn't care less what Morales thought, and she was no snitch, far from it. What difference did it make whose idea it had been? What concerned her most was him talking about his wife in the past tense.

"Is Natalia all right?"

The question irritated him. "I told you, she's gone away to see to a family matter."

That wasn't what he'd said. It seemed as if Morales was trying out the explanation he'd give to anyone asking, and that he didn't care if she noticed the inconsistency, because he had something else to talk to her about.

"I get the impression you're not with us."

"What's that supposed to mean?"

"I think you know what I'm talking about."

"No idea. Why don't you explain it to me."

The door to the living room opened and the tear-stained face of his youngest daughter appeared.

"Daddy, why—"

He turned and silenced her with an imperious gesture.

"But where—"

"Go on, go back inside."

The girl obeyed. Morales turned back to her, stuck with the cold politician's smile he'd given his daughter.

"I'll sum it up for you: your attitude in recent meetings, your aggressiveness towards Germán, your lack of involvement—"

"How can you say that? I've taken part in everything."

"Half-heartedly."

It was payback time for, in everyone else's eyes, not having been enthusiastic enough about the party.

"Your obvious sympathy for the squatters."

"What do you mean?"

"Someone saw you walking with a stranger. Is he one of them?"

"That's none of your business."

"Yes, it is. I am the chairman of the residents' associ—"

"And what does that have to do with my life?"

"More than you think. We are a community in a, shall we say, hostile environment. We have to work as a team. Support each other."

"Spy on each other?"

"Trust each other."

"You mean control each other."

Morales turned round as if he wanted them to carry on the discussion inside the house, but ended up turning a full circle until he was facing her again, hands in pockets.

"Look, I don't feel like you've got the right attitude, honestly. And this thing with Natalia and the stones has just cemented what the other residents were already saying to me."

"Who? What were they saying?"

"That's not the point."

"Tell me straight. What is this thing you need to tell me so urgently?"

"That you're no longer a member of the residents' association."

She was no longer a member of the residents' association.

She was not part of anything.

She lived there. That was all.

That evening, she felt the void when she entered the Moroccans' bar and none of the residents came over to talk to her. They also blanked her in the street. Words and gestures she'd taken for granted before, almost with an arrogant detachment, were now painfully absent.

Four days went by like this, the last of them spent holed up at home. She found that her work brought her some solace while it kept her occupied, but then as soon as she saved her files and turned off the computer, she was alone, trapped in the continuous present. Reading, her other lifeline, failed to distract her mind enough to drown out the unwanted silence around her. She had been left stranded on a tiny boat in the middle of the ocean. She had provisions. She may even have had oars. But she had no map or compass. Just time and space.

She was so immersed in her sudden loneliness that she even forgot about the man and Matías, as if they'd been a mirage on a journey to some far-flung country.

However, like the ghosts of the two dead workmen, they didn't know they were mirages, and they came looking for her.

She saw them materialise on her fourth night of banishment, just as she'd taken the pills from the medicine cabinet and placed them on the balcony table, thinking she would probably need two that night, as well as two Camparis, to get some sleep. At first she heard a rhythmic sound that she did not interpret as footsteps but as the distant stirring of the vanished forest. Then, two figures appeared, in the glow of the lights she had left on all over the house. They stood still in front of the gate. She whistled at them and saw them both look up at the same time and raise a hand to wave. She slipped the pills into her dressing-gown pocket and ran downstairs to open the door. She let them in before anyone might see them, although she didn't know if she cared any more.

"We were worried," he said.

"What a lovely house! May I use your bathroom?" said Matías.

"Of course." She showed him where it was, and the old man disappeared upstairs.

Without Matías there, alone with him, she felt a little intimidated, awkward. He didn't seem that comfortable either.

"I thought that even if you had a lot of work to do, at some point you would come by to see me, to see us..."

"It's been a difficult few days."

"And you don't want to talk about it, right?"

"That's right. Would you like a drink?"

The old man appeared, eyes shining. "Wow, what an amazing bathtub!"

"Yes, that was something my ex-husband wanted."

There was a slightly uncomfortable silence.

"I'll get going," said Matías finally. "It's late."

"Don't you want to stay for a drink?" she offered.

The old man firmly refused. "I'm not used to these things any more. And that's fine. Using the toilet was a treat."

They saw him to the front door.

"Be careful out there," the man said. "Would you like me to come with you?"

"Who showed you the safest route here?"

Matías waved goodbye, left the garden and the saplings behind, and soon melded into the darkness of the night. She briefly lingered in the doorway, straining to hear any neighbours commenting on her visitors, but could hear nothing apart from the wind shaking the eleven poplars.

They went back into the house.

"You didn't tell me what you'd like to drink."

"Do you know what I'd really like?" he said sheepishly. "A bath."

"Only if I can get in with you," she said, surprised by her own forwardness.

They waited impatiently for the enormous bathtub to fill up enough to get in. They undressed slowly, though, like two friends going for a swim in a lake. They held hands as they got in, and sat down facing each other. Their feet were touching. The foamy water came up as far as their hips, leaving his erection out in the open.

"It looks like a periscope," she said, laughing. She bit her bottom lip. Her ex-husband, serious and focused when it came to sex, always got annoyed when she said things like that.

But the man started laughing too. She took off her glasses and straddled him.

She didn't know how long she'd been in the water, resting on his chest, but she was beginning to feel a pleasant sensation of hunger. She'd barely eaten anything in the last few days.

"If we don't get out of the water," he said, "the skin on my fingers is going to peel off."

They got dressed and went down to the kitchen.

"In my former life I was known for making really good fried eggs," he said.

She decided to take this as him offering to cook, not to start talking about the past. Their pasts weren't important; only the present mattered.

A short while later, as she used her bread to mop up every last trace of yolk from her plate, she said to him: "Now it's your turn to ask me what I want."

"Okay. What *do* you want?" He looked at her, grinning.

"I want to spend the night at your place."

"There? Really?"

"Yes. Get me out of here."

They took several more blankets. They did as the old man had said, moving away from the well-lit area and taking a long detour to the uninhabited zone without being seen. It was starting to drizzle. With no doors or windows to close, the air in the apartment was cold and damp. They fell asleep in each other's arms.

33

It happened on the third night she stayed over at his apartment. Friday. Apparently, you shouldn't do things like that if you have work the next day.

They were woken by shouting. They peered out of a window, deciding not to turn on a torch for fear of attracting the attention of the pack of residents, around twenty of them, who had entered the zone and were now making their way noisily down the street.

People with flaming torches. Dazzled by the proximity of the blaze, they couldn't see anything except the burning garden torches they were marching along behind. The heat of the fire scorching their brains, boiling them in its black fumes. Sticking close together lest they turn back into individuals, they egged each other on, elbowing and jabbing like the writhing guts of a single organism.

"Matías!" he said.

Lately, insomnia had taken its toll on the old man, who,

despite the cold nights, spent many hours sitting out on the terrace, next to the metal drum in which he burned wood and paper. Knowing him, he couldn't imagine he'd stay silent when confronted with this mob, and in his mind's eye he saw the figure of the old man, Giordano Bruno in a cardigan, crying out against obscurantism and burning at the top of his building like a funeral pyre.

They threw on their clothes and hurried down to the street. The mass of people had already passed Matías's building, whose rooftop was, fortunately, in darkness. The torches glowed red and yellow, the flames moving between the buildings. That's why they were there too: to burn. But every blaze has to start somewhere, and this mob, this swarm of malevolent fireflies, was being drawn to the only light in the entire zone, the bonfire belonging to the three men who occupied the library. Their own voices masked the dog's frenzied barking until they were suddenly face to face.

The group halted. There were twenty of them, versus three men and a dog. Perhaps some of them, their minds still clouded by the smoke, thought they stood a chance, but most of them must have soon realised that it was not a question of numbers but of ferocity, and that the three men pulling wood from the fire had much more of it, and that any one of those half-charred sticks was far more ferocious than their bamboo garden-centre torches.

And yet inertia steamrolled over intelligence. They had come to burn a block, to eject its occupants, and there they were. One of the settlers stepped forward, followed by three more. Four on four. The others released the dog. The animal had already identified the leader of the pack, who only just raised his arms in time to avoid being bitten in the face.

The rest was very brief. Definitely no epic tale. Furious, clumsy punches at first. Then came the clumsy, frightened punches, and shortly afterwards there was the fleeing. Anyone who'd been in a fight before had almost forgotten it or buried it in the romanticised tales of their youth. The first-timers quickly discovered that in fights there are no rules, and even less choreography; that not only does getting punched hurt, but so does punching.

They discovered other things that didn't happen quite like they do in the movies either, namely that houses don't set on fire when you want them to, and showing up angrily with a jerrycan of petrol isn't enough. Especially when your flaming torch lands in a puddle before you've even had time to unscrew the cap. The wet ground extinguished it, and the jerrycan and the torch were abandoned, leaving a trail of stinking black smoke rising into the air.

Defeated, they returned to the development.

34

Humiliated. Few things are more ridiculous than rage extinguished by a puddle.

The police were not called.

The wounds on Germán's arms were treated in a provincial hospital. They were blamed on a dog that came out of the woods while he was jogging. No one asked which woods.

Everyone else was treated at home, and at the health centre in town the following day.

We'll hire a security company to patrol the area.

When Don Fernando returns and finishes the work, this won't happen any more.

We'll get the fence repaired. Completely. So no one can sneak through.

Because Don Fernando...

Look what your squatter friends have done.

Don Fernando...

Where do you go at night?

*

Where do you go at night?

That's what the note in her letter box said. Who'd seen her? Who was so upset about it that they'd left a note like that? It was handwritten in pencil, pressing down hard.

Where do you go at night?

They couldn't know she'd witnessed the failed attempt to evict the squatters. There was no way they could.

But someone knew that she went to the zone at night, that she left her house as if she were going for a walk, arrived at the roundabout bearing the name of the development, where he was waiting for her, smoking, leaning against the P of Pacheco. When she got there, he put out his cigarette at the foot of the promoter's initial. The gardener must have been raging. They walked along the road to a wasteland where, he told her, Matías's wife was buried. She was equally upset and disturbed to learn that there was another dead body.

"Matías can tell you about that himself."

She still hadn't had a chance to ask him yet. She hadn't had a chance to do much yet, and here she was holding this anonymous letter, these six words of resentment-filled graphite.

It didn't make any difference. That night, she met him again. She hadn't told him anything about what was going on with her and the other residents. She forgot all about them as soon as she left the development; in fact that was why she left.

This time, however, as they walked arm in arm along the road, she told him about the note in the letter box and the way her neighbours were blanking her.

"Then leave."

"I can't."

He didn't answer, he expected more: some form of explanation, maybe justifications. But her story was buried under the sediment of her stubborn refusal to complain about her abandonment and betrayal, and was becoming fossilised by the inertia of her days. She was incapable of shedding a single layer of it.

"I can't. I'm stranded here."

"Stranded? Just pack up and go somewhere else."

She was irritated by his condescending tone and by the fact that he had unknowingly described, in a few words, exactly what her ex-husband had done.

"How easy! Right. So I just pack up and leave? Why didn't I think of that?"

She tried to unlink her arm from his, but he held on to it gently. They had left the roundabout behind them.

"There doesn't seem to be anything tying you to this place," he continued.

"If I could leave, I would have by now. I'm tied. I'm drowning in debt, I have to pay off a mortgage on a house that isn't worth a fifth of what I paid for it, and I can't sell either—"

"But—"

"I don't want to talk about it."

Only the present mattered and, just as she respected him not telling her about his past, she hoped he'd respect her desire to not stir hers up either. Only the present counted. Not even the future was important. She was about to tell him that when he stopped abruptly.

"No? So for you this is just about going on walks and shagging a squatter?"

She pulled away from him sharply. "What did you say?"

"If you don't want to talk to me about anything, what do you come here for? A fling to pass the time? Something to tell your friends on the development about?"

"Didn't I just tell you I'm all on my own here?"

Turning away from him, she walked off into the darkness, propelled by anger. Not hearing his voice behind her, she grew sadder with every step. He didn't go after her.

She got back to her house.

Where do you go at night?

35

"Isn't she coming?"

Matías had been waiting for them in his apartment, to drink a couple of rums and have a chat.

"No."

"What happened?"

He hoped the story would prove him right, but every line of it made him wrong, made him a coward, made him cruel.

The old man shook his head and tutted, both of which irritated him.

"Is there something you want to say?"

"Yes. That you're a fool. What you've done to her, you already tried with me."

"It's not the same thing."

"A variation on a theme, then. But essentially... Well, you know what you're doing. And now you'll be able to leave."

Without saying goodbye, he left Matías's apartment. He

would take a long walk through the fields before going back to his own.

He was tempted to walk near her house, but he resisted. He had driven her away, Matías was right about that. It was as if he'd seen a chance to break away from her and had taken it. He had enough to worry about with the old man.

Yep, he actually was a fool.

The crunching of the grass beneath his feet kept time with his footsteps. Probably the same dry, brittle sound that a cicada would make if stepped on. He started whistling, but the songs sounded unenthusiastic. Whistling was for fools.

Even with the extra blankets, he shivered all night long. He wasn't sure which was colder, the air or the ground.

36

Work, blessed work, came to the rescue. It came in the form of an internal company email asking for someone to replace a colleague who was on leave, for one of their projects with partners in South Korea. A financial incentive was being offered. But so far no one had shown much interest in the job, because there was an issue: the seven-hour time difference that made it necessary to work at night. *Perfect*, she replied. *When can I start?*

Can you start this evening?

Of course she could.

Before her first night shift, she had run for an hour through the streets of the development. The weather had changed, it was cold as soon as it got dark, so nobody was out walking or in their gardens; the windows were lit but closed, and life had moved indoors. She went through the different parts of the development, past the villas, then the apartments, zigzagging through the streets, and reached the part where there were fewer windows with lights on. She avoided Germán's street. A figure out running in the dark was too tempting for the barrel of a shotgun that had been lying in wait for weeks. She didn't venture into the fields either; she didn't even go near the park that ended at the roundabout. It was not the darkness that frightened her, but the possibility of bumping into him.

At midnight she started her workday. The vampire shift. The work was intense, formal presentations, long sessions in English. It was not the first time she'd worked with foreign programmers, but it was her first time as a representative of the company. A few breaks, one of them for a short Korean lunch. She finished just before 8 a.m. Outside, the day started off windy. She gave the plants a good watering. It had been days since a drop of rain had fallen, and the wind was drying them out even more. She secured the hose firmly, so it wouldn't budge with the gusts of wind, and folded up the washing line in the back garden. She positioned the chair and table on the balcony so they wouldn't bang against each other. Then she took a quick shower, greeted the eleven poplars, wishing them a good day, and pulled down all the blinds until the house was in total darkness. She took a pill, without Campari. Campari is not a drink for nine in the morning. Earplugs in. Lights off. With all her senses dimmed, she fell asleep.

37

What he was doing was dangerous, irrational, feverish. He was casting aside the precautions he'd learned throughout the entire time he'd been there and was walking in broad daylight through the streets of the development. It was just after 10 a.m. Those who had to leave for work or school, or to go shopping, had already left.

Most of them. A woman behind the wheel of a blue SUV gave him an odd look as she drove past. He could feel her eyeing him in the rear-view mirror until the sound of the engine was out of earshot.

A man, Moroccan or Algerian, sweeping the street in front of a bar, stopped the rhythmic scraping of the broom to let him go past. He did not carry on sweeping afterwards. Again he felt eyes on the back of his head, even when he rounded a corner and was out of sight.

He felt a sudden wave of dizziness and had to grab hold of a nearby garden fence. A hurried pitter-patter behind the dense, meticulously kept hedge, and a growl. The animal waited for him to start walking again before starting to bark. Perhaps in solidarity; perhaps out of cowardice.

Finally, he reached the street where the house was located, next door to one that had been empty for some time. Hers also had all the blinds pulled down tight, like the eyes of someone in deep sleep. He made his way round the outside of the house. On the other side, facing the fields, there were no chinks either. He peered through the garden fence. The wind shook the plants. The ground was drenched, like when someone knows they're going to be gone for several days. He looked up at the balcony. Empty. Her bedroom blind lowered. He rang the doorbell. The cicadas, as if they'd been poised, waiting for the Greek chorus's entrance, struck up behind him.

SHE'S-NOT-IN-SHE'S-NOT-IN.

He rang the doorbell again.

Only the chorus responded.

SHE'S-NOT-IN-SHE'S-NOT-IN.

One last try.

GET-LOST-GET-LOST-GET-LOST, said the cicadas.

He turned away. Another dizzy spell. He grabbed hold of the rough trunk of one of the trees that marked the end of the development like a dotted line. He breathed until he felt his head and heart recover.

This time he made his way back across the fields. He was exhausted and thirsty when he got to his apartment. After gulping down some water, he got into bed. He didn't remember taking off his shoes, but one of the many times he woke up he noticed that he was barefoot and night was falling.

38

She slept for about six hours. She'd already been warned that for the first few days she'd experience a kind of jet lag. She took the advice of a colleague and, despite how windy it was, moved the chair and table onto the balcony and had her breakfast out there. It was 4 p.m. At that time of day there was no chance of the phantom forest making an appearance. The light left no room for doubt. The poplars were poplars, the fields were bare surfaces, and in the background, nothing more than hills.

And yet she felt unsettled for some reason. She put the feeling of uneasiness down to the jet lag, to her hectic first night at work, to the lingering drowsiness the pills sometimes left her with, to a lack of sleep, to the wind. She sensed something moving to her right. She looked in that direction. There was a shadow looming beside the house. Someone was approaching.

She leaned forward, and the metal legs of the chair

grated on the floor. The shadow stopped and stood against the side wall of the house, still.

Putting her cup down on the table, she got up from her chair, this time without making a sound, and peered over the railing. She couldn't make out who it was. The sun was behind her, casting her shadow on the pavement too. The other shadow shook, as if flinching. It moved. It receded until it disappeared.

She ran downstairs and out into the back garden, but whoever it was had already vanished.

39

In the morning he woke up with a fuzzy head. He had hardly any coffee left but didn't want to ask the old man to help him with the shopping, or even to go with him. If he called him a fool one more time, he would smash his face in.

Fool. Matías had called him a fool. It was an older man's word. His grandfather used to use the word for people who were stupid, clumsy; cowards, too. He couldn't remember ever saying it himself. Perhaps it was a word that lay dormant and was only activated in your seventies. Well, he wasn't going to wait. He wasn't that confident about reaching his seventies, either. "Yes, I'm a fool," he said after clearing his throat with an almost transparent coffee.

The tingling in his legs ordered him to start walking. His body demanded long, aimless walks. However, his knees felt cottony, and he wasn't sure they could get him back if he went too far into the fields.

He spent the day wandering the streets, hoping not to run into Matías or any of the others who lived round there. The wind changed temperature with every gust. Summer and autumn were in the midst of a territorial battle, but instead of fighting each other they were enjoying making him go from sweating to shivering. He took refuge in the house of the two ghosts and sat on the floor with his back against some parched pallets. He started quietly reciting names until he nodded off.

A banging noise from inside the structure woke him. Something, a brick, a piece of wood or concrete, had fallen somewhere. He felt a cold hand tapping the back of his neck, like fingers drumming. He stood up slowly. His legs were numb, his arm joints stiff. He tried to do some exercises to warm up, but when he moved his heart was beating too fast. It was already dark, and the Dominican's shift would start soon. He had killed the day so he could go and buy coffee.

If the walk to the petrol station seemed long, the distance doubled on the way back; his legs were heavy, his arms ached, sometimes his eyesight failed, blurring if he tried to focus on a specific point. He plodded up the stairs to his apartment, wearily greeted the little play kitchen, sadly greeted the one-armed plastic doll she had left, or perhaps had left for him, and fell heavily onto the jumble of blankets that was his bed.

He dreamed that water was running through the pipes of the building and that hundreds of tadpoles were swimming inside it. The little bodies with massive heads moved frantically, looking for the way out.

Go, go, go, your legs are starting to emerge.

A viscous churning pressed together in a blind race.

Go, go, go, you're already growing lungs.

A bend in a pipe. A blockage.

Push, push.

Some pushed with the tails they still had, others with their tiny budding arms; the most terrified ones already had their frog legs.

Go, go, go, your lungs will start to need air soon.

Suffocation.

40

The faces were disappearing from the screen one by one. The meeting with her Korean colleagues was finished; she took off her headphones.

People who prefer night work always talk about the quiet, the absence of distracting noises. They never say anything about the intensity that sounds acquire at night. The hum of the fridge, the notched beats propelling the hands of a wall clock, wood creaking somewhere in the house, a crumpled piece of paper uncrumpling in the wastepaper basket. The wind shaking the poplars. And footsteps.

It must be an insomniac walking around.

It was 3 a.m., the start of that portion of the night which tortures those who can't sleep, those who have already lost all hope of sleep and know that even if it deigns to come, it will be insufficient. She imagined them wandering the streets of the development in their checked flannel pyjamas, shuffling along in their slippers, squinting in the bright light of the street lamps.

But the feet that were passing her house did not shuffle, they stepped firmly, with sturdy soles. She got up and went to the window overlooking the street. She couldn't see anyone. She opened the door. The footsteps moved away in the direction of the empty terraced house on the left.

"Hello?"

Someone ran off.

For the first time since moving to the development, she locked the gates with a key. For the rest of the night she worked with every single light on in the house.

41

Footsteps.

Footsteps gently approaching.

He half opened his eyes.

The guardian rat had turned into a huge bug that was prowling around his room.

"I haven't got any cheese for you, my friend," he said, closing his eyes. The scarce sunlight filtering into the room hurt them.

"What's that?" the rat replied, standing still.

His eyelids burned. So did his forehead and his hands. His feet were ice-cold. They felt very far away.

"You can't eat me. We've talked and I've got a name, but I won't tell you what it is," he mumbled.

He tucked his hands into his armpits, just in case; it's always the fingers that rats start gnawing at first.

42

To avoid changing her sleep pattern, she had to stay awake on her night off from Sunday into Monday. She would take a long walk beforehand. She didn't want to see anyone, so she avoided the streets of the development. Walking across the fields, she came to the large park. There was still water in the central lake from the recent downpours. It was about half a metre deep around the big central mound, intended to be a miniature island for tiny boats to circle aimlessly, like fish in an aquarium. Although she'd probably seen it on the plans for the development, she couldn't recall what was supposed to be on the island. A Neptune, she bet, huge and muscular, with Pacheco's face.

On the paths that were marked out, the compacted earth still prevented the onward march of the vegetation, but this was not the case with the stones. In the middle of one of the paths she found a stone marked with a thick blue line. Where was Natalia? She hadn't come back to the development. Or maybe she had but they were keeping her in the house, the way that in rural areas they used to hide away mentally ill or disabled relatives. She'd also not seen Sergio Morales since he'd banished her from the residents' association.

She picked up the stone. It fitted perfectly in her hand. She flung it hard, watched to see where it landed, and headed that way. To her surprise, it was easy to find, because it had landed with the blue mark facing upwards, as if it wanted to keep on playing. She threw it again. And found it again. She repeated the throw. This time, she held on to the stone after picking it up again; she had a better idea. She went to the end of the park, to the statue of Fernando Pacheco's grandfather. Planting her feet firmly on the ground, she threw the stone at his face as hard as she could. One forceful whack, and the stone and the tip of his nose fell to the ground in unison. She picked them up and, with one in each hand, jumped around the statue in victory.

"Take that! On the first go!"

The gardener, that snitch, he'd lose his fucking mind over this.

She carried on dancing triumphantly on the roundabout. There were no cigarette butts. Either he hadn't been there, or the gardener had already done his job.

To shake off the instant sadness she felt at remembering him, she started walking around Pacheco's name, touching the huge letter *P* each time.

"Gimme a *P*! *P*! Gimme an *A*! *A*!"

A sudden fear stopped her in her tracks. What if someone spotted her right at that second? The road was deserted and so was the avenue. But what if?

It was getting dark. She had to go home. And she would take the most direct route.

Placing the stone and piece of nose at the foot of the statue, she left.

She made her way through the development like someone crossing enemy territory, fast-paced, eyes fixed straight ahead. In the streets where the large villas were, she walked down the middle of the road. A few of the houses had cars parked in front of them: visitors from the outside world. The settlers always parked their cars in their own garages. Voices and the smell of meat on the barbecue.

As she went into her house, she left a trail of lights on behind her. She created an artificial day to protect her from sleep, and from the vague fear she could not shake off.

Plans. She needed to make plans for the night. To create a structure that would keep her going. She would cook something with a complicated recipe. Then, several episodes of a series. Then some gaming.

As she was alone, she could do all of that without headphones. She didn't want to be isolated from her surroundings as she gamed with other people from all over the world. She had pulled down all the blinds, the doors were locked, the lights were on. In order not to leave anything to the imagination, she'd checked under the bed and looked inside the wardrobe. And even in the kitchen cupboards. What did she expect to find there? A killer doll?

She realised how suggestible she was being and managed to laugh at herself, which expelled her fears from the house. Fear and humour have never got along.

But when the doorbell rang at three in the morning, she screamed involuntarily. 3 a.m. again. The hour of hopeless insomniacs. The time of night when someone was prowling the streets of the development. She froze.

The doorbell rang again more insistently. Then came some knocking.

She got up and went to the front door.

Another ring, more knocking.

She didn't dare to look out of the peephole. That would give her away.

As if the person on the other side could sense her presence, they didn't ring the doorbell again but this time knocked gently.

"Open up, please. It's me."

She peeped out then. The fisheye glass showed the distorted image of Matías standing very still, as if posing for a photo. She opened the door.

"Grab everything you have in the medicine cabinet and come with me, please."

She ushered Matías inside, glancing outside before she shut the door. The street lights illuminated the empty road.

After that, she went upstairs to the bathroom and emptied the cabinet where she kept her medicines.

"We'd better go out the back," she said to Matías.

He had also come round the back way, although to knock on her door he'd had to venture near the houses: "I thought if I rang the other bell you'd be scared."

Matías told her that the man was sick. He'd gone to see him because it had been a while, which was odd, and had found him lying in bed, raving about tadpoles and rats.

"What's wrong with him?" she asked, as they walked away from the well-lit area.

"Fever."

"Fever's a symptom, not an illness."

"I hope pedantry is just a symptom too," the old man replied with a laugh.

They walked the rest of the way in silence. They entered the zone through a narrow gap they both knew about.

The person who didn't know about it was whoever had been following them without them noticing. They heard a thud, followed by a muffled groan. They both instantly stopped. There was a creak of metal: someone was struggling with the fence.

"Come on!" said Matías under his breath.

They turned a corner, and she followed him along the pavement covered in rubble until they reached the door of the last block on the street. It was covered with metal sheeting, which gave way when Matías pushed it. They went inside, and the old man sealed it shut. He took her hand to guide her through the building. They crossed what must have been the entrance hall, and found the staircase. Matías moved confidently through the space. She allowed herself to be led. When they reached the first floor, they saw a light moving along the street. They peered out of the window frame. Their pursuer was lighting up the ground with the torch on his phone. They moved away from the window in case he shone the beam on them. But she glimpsed that he was carrying a lengthy object. Was he armed?

43

Cold. A cold that seeped in through any minuscule gap in the layers of blankets. He bent his legs up, tucked his hands between his knees. Beneath that shell, his body began to warm up. But the growing pressure on his bladder prevented him from dropping off. He tried to ignore it; maybe he could fall asleep before it was too urgent. In the end, he had no choice but to get up. His legs were shaking so much that he wasn't sure how he would get down to the latrine in the next building, let alone back up the stairs.

Coming out of his apartment, he went to the one furthest away on that floor. He didn't dare go near the balcony opening, so he urinated out of a window instead, feeling like a teenage lout. As he fastened his trousers, he chuckled softly. He started shivering, as if the laughter had rid his body of all the heat accumulated under the blankets. He returned to his apartment but before he entered the room he was stopped by a sound coming from outside. Someone was walking along the street. He wondered if it was her. Actually, he wished it was her. He looked out. A person was moving along the middle of the street, shining their phone torch at the ground. It was a man. And he was armed. Even from a distance he could make out the barrel of the gun he was clutching, as if afraid of being ambushed.

They'd found him. How?

The man walked past. He could not work out which of his three former colleagues it was.

His legs were failing him. Running away was not an option in his condition. Whoever was out there roaming the street would not find him, at least not that night. He crawled into bed and covered himself with the blankets, cursing his lack of foresight for not leaving them in a way that kept in the heat. He ducked his head underneath to muffle his cough. It was a sudden, frail, rasping sound, like an old man. How had they found him? How had he slipped up? The pain constricted his chest and throat, so swollen he struggled to even swallow.

Everything was quiet again. The only sound was his wheezing, as if his chest was full of pipes like an organ. He dozed off.

He woke abruptly. Someone was talking to him, asking him something. *You keep hold of it?*

"No," he said, then realised the voice was the bubbling in his lungs.

He lay there with his heart racing painfully until the fever plunged him back into sleep.

44

Motionless and silent, they waited until they could no longer hear the man's footsteps.

They went outside. She walked ahead and stopped in the middle of the street, realising Matías was not close behind. He'd got distracted by carefully sliding the metal sheet across, closing it like it was the front door to a house.

"What are you doing?"

"I lived here with Teresa," he whispered.

They moved slowly, ears pricked for any sounds that might alert them to the man's presence. Finally they reached the entrance to the block and went upstairs in silence.

"I'm armed," said a tremulous voice. "If you come near me, I'll blow you away."

"Come off it!" Matías replied without slowing his pace.

They found him sitting up in bed wrapped in blankets. The room stank of sweat, of the breath of a sick man.

"Look what's happened to this fool since you left," said Matías, his voice full of fondness.

The lump under the blankets grunted and then started coughing. "Go away," he said between coughs. "It's not safe to be near me."

"He's delirious again. Have you got anything for a fever?"

"Aspirin, ibuprofen, or paracetamol," she said, taking three packs out of her bag.

While Matías hesitated and the lump went on coughing, she decided on ibuprofen. She took out two pills. "Water," she said to Matías, who filled a glass.

The two of them approached the bed. In the palm of her hand, she held the pills; Matías held the glass. They knelt down at his bedside. She was about to comment that they looked like a couple of low-budget Magi, but she resisted.

He reached one hand out of the bundle, took the pills, and swallowed them with difficulty. The light from the phone revealed his shining, sunken eyes, his greasy hair. She touched his forehead. It was burning up. When she went to move her hand away, he held on to it. A loving gesture, perhaps, or simply to relieve the fever.

"Please go away."

"Do you have anything else we can give him?" Matías asked. Both knees had creaked as he stood up.

"I've got antibiotics, but they're out of date."

"What could happen to him if he takes them?"

"I have no idea."

"Well, let's give them to him then."

Matías filled the glass again. She freed her hand from his grip, rummaged around in her bag, and pulled out the packet. They gave him two of those as well.

"Get out of here or they'll kill you," he said. "You too, Matías. They're coming for me. They're coming for me."

He babbled some garbled story about money, corruption, conspiracy, a bag, some gloves, names that tumbled out of his mouth because he was falling asleep as he was talking. The only thing keeping him awake was the fear. Because they'd found him, he said. He was talking, no doubt, about the armed man.

"He's coming for me. You have to go!"

"You need to rest," she said as she tried to fluff up the pillow caked in dried sweat. Then she gently encouraged him to lie down again.

"Go away, please," he said, lying back on the bed. "You too, Matías." He reached for her hand and squeezed it tightly. "They'll kill us all," he said before falling asleep.

His breathing was regular but noisy, crackly. A bonfire inside his lungs.

Matías insisted on walking her back. "Did you get any of that?" he asked.

"No."

"But we really did see that man."

She understood what he was trying to say; it was not some fever-induced fantasy.

"Do you know why he's here?"

"No, but he's got a bag full of money. And a fear of the police. Although everyone living in the zone is afraid of the police, to be fair."

They walked on in silence, too tired to indulge in speculation. They parted just before they reached her house. The light radiating from the development made that final stretch safer.

"Maybe it's best if you stay away," said Matías, and gave her a kiss on the cheek as he left.

"We'll see."

She went into her house.

The Korean clients were slightly peeved about not being able to get hold of her. Aware of their sense of technological superiority, she blamed it on the poor quality of her own internet connection, which seemed to appease them. Then she tried to get on with her work as usual. She didn't give them any extra time, because that would have been an admission of guilt.

At the end of the day, she spent an hour searching the internet. The symptoms opened up too many possibilities and, above all, the term "death rattle" appeared too often. It was a medical term, yes, but it also seemed like a bird of ill omen. Expired antibiotics would not do him any particular harm, but they might not have any effect.

She went to the mini mart and bought several cartons of chicken soup, isotonic drinks, bread, chocolate, a pack of sliced ham, and some yogurt. With this combination of all the things her mother would feed her when she was ill or which she craved on a hangover, she headed back into the fenced-off zone. She looked around to see if she could detect any sign of the armed man, although she didn't think he'd be walking around in broad daylight.

After entering the apartment, she peeked inside the bedroom. He was sleeping.

His breathing was agitated and the noises, the little clicks that went with it, made her think of "death rattle" in the plural, a flock of death rattles, evil birds that always flew with death in tow. She went over to him and touched his forehead. He woke with a start. She saw fear in his eyes, and instantly regretted scaring him.

"What are you doing here?" he said, then had to prop himself up on one side because he was coughing so hard.

"I brought you a few things," she said, pointing to the bag on the floor and feeling like a grown-up Red Riding Hood.

"Go away! It's not safe here." He struggled until he was sitting upright amongst the blankets.

"But—"

"What if someone saw you come in?"

She realised that Little Red Riding Hood, adult or not, is actually not the brightest spark because she lets slip to the wolf that Grandma is ill and all alone in her little house in the woods.

"No one followed me," she said, less convincingly than she would have liked. She stood up and took the isotonic drink out of the bag. "Before I go, take your medication with this."

Again, two ibuprofen and two antibiotic tablets, which he gulped down without taking his eyes off her.

"And now you have to go," he said.

"But—"

"Please. You don't know what they're capable of."

"What if they find you?"

"That's my problem. But you—"

"I could call the police."

"Please don't make it more complicated."

Bending down, she kissed him on the head, the way he had on their first walk together. "I brought you some soup and other things too... for you to eat... and... well, I'm going."

She left without turning to look at him.

Pushed away again. This time, though, she wouldn't accept it.

She did not have the full story, but she knew enough to understand that he was on the run from the law. That's why she wouldn't call the police, but she wouldn't leave him alone either. Whatever are you going to do, Little Red Riding Hood?

Absurd ideas began flitting through her head. How was she supposed to protect him from a guy with a gun, someone who was hunting him down to kill him?

The dry breeze whipped up dust from the fields. Not a cloud in sight. The light bothered her eyes. She could feel the exhaustion with every step.

She got home and, going through the motions, opened her letter box.

Junk mail – even out there they got junk mail – a letter from the bank, which had systematically been ignoring her requests to go paperless, and a handwritten note: WHERE DO YOU GO AT NIGHT?

It was like a slap in the face. Immediately, all her tiredness was gone. She couldn't stay at home; she had to keep moving. Grabbing the letter, she bunched her keys in her fist as if she were holding a blade, and set off.

Where are you going? Where do you go at night? Where are you going? What do you care? I'm just moving, I'm not going anywhere. Step after step, aimlessly, through streets that were, as always, practically deserted. Occasionally she heard voices or music coming from a house. There was a little more activity in the area where the first apartments were, but not much. A woman went into the mini mart. Through the glass door of the hairdresser's, she saw someone having their hair washed.

She went to the Moroccans' bar. She planned to have a coffee and see if they'd taken her advice and bought little plastic skewers for the pinchos.

In the end, she did neither of those things.

At the melodious fruit machine, Germán was putting a coin into the slot. In his other hand was an almost-empty beer glass. The machine swallowed the coin and trilled another tune but did not release a prize. Germán turned to see who'd come in, and was clearly startled. He stared at the handwritten note she was clutching. He immediately turned back to the machine but the coin quivered in the air, refusing to enter the slot. His eyes didn't want to obey him either, and he glanced sideways at the note she was now holding up to show him.

"This," she said, "is this your doing?"

"I don't know what the fuck you're talking about."

"Yes, you do. You wrote this. You've been spying on me."

As she said it, the penny dropped.

She realised that the armed man wasn't looking for *him*, he had been following *her*. It wasn't the big bad wolf; it was someone who thought he was the noble hunter.

Germán had managed to get the coin into the slot. The machine played a mocking little melody to tell him that he'd lost and that he was losing.

"And it's you who's been hanging around my house."

"I don't hang around your house. I patrol."

"Patrol?"

"The other day, Yolanda saw a stranger loitering around here. Maybe he was one of your new friends."

As he said this, he looked around. He was saying it for the benefit of the people in there, who she'd not even noticed as she came in. At a table near the back, Beatriz Puértolas was having coffee with three other women who lived in the apartment blocks. They'd stopped talking and were now watching them. So was a young man sitting alone at a table by the window, who was the son of someone who lived in the villas, although she couldn't remember who. Only Dounia behind the bar seemed oblivious to the conversation, busily loading glasses into the dishwasher.

"So you're the self-proclaimed sheriff, are you? Patrolling the houses of helpless maidens. To protect them." She looked over at the women's table. "I mean, I hope it's to protect them, anyway."

She turned on her heel and left the bar. But before the slow-closing door could fully shut, a sentence slipped through.

"Where do you go at night?"

She came back in, crumpled up the piece of paper, and flung it at his face.

45

Matías went up three times a day to feed him. Cartons of soup heated over the stove, some sliced bread. Then the liturgy of ibuprofen and antibiotics. They hardly spoke. It was still too much of an effort for him, and Matías seemed preoccupied. But that didn't stop the old man from getting angry every time he asked him not to come back, not to put himself in danger by looking after him.

"They're coming for me."
"Yes, you've already told me."
"They're dangerous."
"Eat your soup while it's still hot."
"You don't know what they're like."
"No, and I don't need to. Go on, swallow your pill."

Swallow is what he did with everything he was given. At first he could barely get the tablets to go down. His body was a jumble of blocked pipes. When he dozed off, he could hear muddy footsteps inside himself.

It was much worse when he fell asleep. Then they came back. Their voices as clear as if they were whispering in his ear. "You keep hold of it," Ibáñez told him. Ibáñez's gloved hands gripped his throat. The other two watched and laughed. Medina shook the keys in the air at Luján. Gómez clapped his hands and sang "Jingle Bells" as he stomped his feet on the floor. He would wake up coughing and with a cramp in his leg.

They were there. They were looking for him in the development. If they had got into Luján's apartment, they would have seen that he'd been hiding out there. They might not notice that he'd taken blankets and towels and other belongings; they wouldn't know. Perhaps they assumed he was long gone by now. But one of them had been hunting around the zone. They suspected something. What if they ran into Matías? The old man was smart; he knew how to hide. He remembered how, at first, he'd been watching him without him realising.

What if she came back and they saw her?

Fucking emotions! He was more afraid for them than for himself.

There was only one solution: he would leave as soon as he got his strength back. He would leave the money to her so she could get out of there too. But what about Matías? The old man wanted to stay and be buried alongside his wife. He would have to hand over the mission to the Dominican: he'd leave him some money too.

He curled up in a ball, shrouding himself completely beneath the mound of stolen blankets.

Someone uncovered him.

It was Matías. "What's wrong?" said the old man. "Are you crying?"

46

That night, after only a few hours of chemical-induced sleep, she worked with the blinds half open. If Germán was watching her, he'd know she was at home. To make sure she was seen, she also stepped out into the garden during every break. She couldn't say why, but on one of these outings she noticed that he was nearby, snooping. And armed?

As long as he was spying on her, she would stay away from the zone. So although she wanted to go and tell him that he shouldn't be afraid of the men who were looking for him, she chose not to go near him. Germán was a hunter; he knew how to follow his prey. Last time he'd given himself away because he was unfamiliar with the terrain, but he'd probably studied it since then. Seeing the empty shelves in the bathroom cupboard, she was reminded that Matías would be stuffing him full of ibuprofen and out-of-date antibiotics.

The following night, she repeated the routine of regularly going out into the street.

At 4 a.m., mug of coffee in hand, she walked a little way up the pavement to stretch her legs. As she was about to head back inside, she heard a rustling coming from the garden of the vacant house. Under any other circumstances she would have thought it was an animal prowling around, the advance guard of the vole invasion, but she knew it was Germán hiding there.

Just then, a light came on in one of the terraced houses opposite. Without thinking, she smashed the mug on the floor and started to scream.

"Who's there? Who's there?"

The window that had lit up was immediately flung open. Someone peered out. She approached the spot where the noise had come from.

"Who's there? What are you doing hiding in my garden?"

Another light came on opposite, allowing her to see Germán's stunned face. He was sitting cross-legged behind the hedge. He was trying to get up but apparently he'd been hiding there for a long time, perhaps so long he'd drifted off, and his legs weren't playing ball.

"What's going on?" someone shouted out of the window.

"There's someone hiding in the garden," she shouted back. "Call the police."

"For fuck's sake! It's me!" Germán yelled, standing up with great difficulty.

"Is it a tramp?" asked the voice from the window.

"I don't know," she answered without turning around. She smiled at Germán, whose jacket was snagged on some branches.

More lights, more voices preventing Germán's answer from being heard.

"No, no! It's me!" He sounded like a child ripping off their disguise, genuinely frightened because they think the grown-ups don't recognise them.

Someone who lived in the next street came round the corner, wearing pyjamas and a big fluffy dressing gown. "What's going on?"

"Don't call the police, it's me!" shouted Germán, still from behind the hedge.

"What?"

"An intruder!"

"Call the police."

"I already have."

More lights, more people, more voices.

"It's me. Germán."

"What?"

"Who's Germán?"

Then she saw that Germán was trying to conceal something with his foot.

"He's got a gun!"

Shouts, lights, voices.

Police sirens.

Later, after over an hour of trying to explain what had happened, statements. Excuses.

"But... she's the one... she's the one sneaking into the zone at night," Germán argued, with his newly acquired status of intruder.

The two police officers, ill-tempered and half asleep, had no patience for his cryptic explanations. All that mattered was the loaded shotgun, which he claimed he was trying to protect his neighbours with. It was taken away and handed over to the civil guards who showed up later, around dawn.

She'd definitely got him off her back for a while. Even so, she needed to be cautious; too many people had heard Germán's accusations.

47

"Keep still, for Christ's sake!"

"But she likes the beard though."

"This isn't a beard, it's just dirt."

Matías had taken him to the living room, made him take off his shirt, and wiped his body with a damp, soapy cloth. He shuddered every time the cold rag touched him, but he let him do it, because Matías kept saying it was removing the scab of sickness.

"You can do your nether regions yourself, kid."

Kid. He liked that word as much as the smell of soap. It was another old-mannish word, like fool.

Matías's sons were probably his age, they were men. But he was a kid Matías was looking after. He gave him medicine, fed him, went with him to pee out of the window, and now he wanted to give him a shave. And he was a kid, afraid she'd come back and see him beardless. Because now they'd found out from the Dominican that the armed man was some lunatic from the settlement, at some point she would come back. But why hadn't she yet? What if he really had pushed her away?

"Tilt your head back slightly."

He did as he was told.

"What are the tadpoles up to?"

"Most of them are gone."

The razor glided over his right cheek. As long as he was a kid, Matías's hand would remain steady.

48

The message began by saying that perhaps they'd been unfair to her. She didn't read on. No apology should contain a "perhaps". She deleted the email from Sergio Morales.

First, she ran through all her morning rituals after her night of work: she switched off the computer, took a shower, watered the plants, lowered the blinds. Then she left the house. She walked through the development, waving wordlessly to anyone who greeted her from their garden or on the street. She didn't stop to talk to anyone, not even Raquel, whom she saw near the Moroccan bar and who slowed down as she approached, took a breath when they came face to face, ready to talk, but then had to let it out in a long sigh because she passed Raquel without even looking up.

She left the various zones behind her: the finished apartment blocks, the partially inhabited, the practically uninhabited. She reached the tarmac road and kept on walking until she found the first hole in the fence. The fridge, belly up, was already turning yellow.

The building's entrance gate was closed, but she was able to open it without it clanking. Good. She reached the inner room. She found him asleep. He looked much better than he'd done three days ago. He'd even shaved. The room no longer smelled of sickness.

She took off all her clothes and lay down beside him. He woke up, startled.

"Don't be scared, I'm not a giant rat."

"What are you doing here?"

"I've come to sleep."

She laid her head on the pillow and covered herself with the blankets. His hands began to roam over her body, as if he needed to check that she was really there. She noticed his growing excitement, but all she wanted to do was sleep. She was so tired. There would be time for all that later. She just wanted to sleep. At last. Really sleep.

49

"I wasn't sure if you were enjoying it or dying on me," she said.

They'd just had rather disastrous sex. He didn't have the strength to be on top; he couldn't breathe if she was; and when they were on their sides, his ribs hurt.

As the daylight faded outside in the street, they lay there sleepily, holding each other. His face was pressed into her neck. She could feel the faint prickle of his stubble.

"What day is it today?" he asked.

"Wednesday."

"Tonight I want to show you something."

"I work nights. We can see whatever it is you want to show me another day. Tomorrow."

"No. It has to be Wednesday."

"Next week then."

"No."

He lay on his side with his head propped on his hand,

looking at her, his eyes glittering. She touched his forehead. He didn't have a fever.

"I can ask for a few hours."

She sent a text message, requesting three hours off. As she never gave any explanations, they didn't ask her for any. As she'd never let them down before either, they agreed to it.

Shortly before midnight they left the zone. The darkness was absolute.

"The day I arrived there was a new moon too."

Arm in arm, they walked across the fields, to avoid the road. He was still weak and they had to stop to let him catch his breath. They got to the roundabout.

They crouched down behind the stone letters.

"It can't be long now," he said.

"What are we doing here?" she asked.

"Just wait, you're in for a surprise."

Although they were alone, they spoke in whispers.

They'd been there for about ten minutes when they heard a noise in the park.

"Now?"

"No, that must be an animal or something. What we're waiting for has to come from the other direction."

It appeared at around half-past midnight.

First, the headlights of a vehicle approaching. The car, a Mercedes, stopped a few metres from the roundabout. The lights went off and the driver got out.

He squeezed her hand.

The man in the Mercedes switched on a torch and started to walk towards the statue. As he passed the stone letters, she peered out to look. "Is that... Fernando Pacheco?" she whispered in his ear.

He nodded.

Then, from behind the pedestal, emerged the figure of another man. Fernando Pacheco stopped and shone the torch at him. The man was carrying a shovel. "It's the gardener," she said.

What the hell was he doing there?

She remembered the stone she'd used to break the statue's nose, and the cigarette butts which absolutely infuriated him. He had probably hidden there to try and catch the smoker.

But now the man's expression was one of astonishment, of wonder, as he came face to face with Pacheco, who, having got over this initial shock, trained the torch beam on him.

"Who are you?"

"Don Fernando? Is that really you?"

Pacheco nodded and, instantly, the gardener dropped the shovel on the ground and fell to his knees in front of the developer.

"What the hell are you doing, man?"

"You've come back! I knew you would! You've returned, Don Fernando!" Still kneeling, the gardener shuffled towards Pacheco and flung his arms round his legs.

"Let go of me! What are you doing? What do you want?"

The gardener was clinging to the developer's legs so tightly that he staggered and kicked out to try and free himself from the arms that imprisoned him.

"I said let go!"

The gardener was on all fours now, but still in a state of ecstasy. He reared up, lifting his hands in the air as if praising a deity. Blinking, because Pacheco was shining the torch right in his eyes.

"You've returned!"

Without turning it off, Pacheco put the torch in his jacket pocket and took a step towards the gardener. "Who the fuck are you?"

"I work for you, for the community, but most of all for you. Don't you remember me? I shook your hand at the opening of the development, you told me I was doing a good job."

"I've shaken a lot of hands in my life."

"But you were talking to me, I introduced you to my wife, you told me I was doing a good job—"

"I say that to a lot of people."

"But Don Fernando..." The gardener, still on his knees, had lowered his arms. He shuffled forward again, like a penitent. Two steps. Pacheco took the same number of steps backwards.

The gardener tried to embrace his knees again. Pacheco jumped back. "What are you doing? Leave me alone! Are you crazy?"

The gardener hung his head. "I've been waiting for you for so, so long..."

"Why the hell are you crying? Come on, man, get up and stop making an arse of yourself." Pacheco waved his hand contemptuously and laughed. He had a cruel laugh; even living in hiding, he hadn't lost that. Suddenly he stopped laughing, turned his back on the gardener, and walked back towards his car.

The gardener raised his head, stood up, grabbed the shovel, and, leaning on it like a crutch, he went after the developer. With his free hand he grabbed Pacheco by the collar of his jacket. "No. You can't leave again."

Pacheco, scared, broke into a run, slipping out of his jacket and leaving the gardener holding the inert garment. He hurled it to the ground and followed Pacheco, who was struggling to open the car door.

"You can't leave. You can't leave me here again."

Pacheco swung a punch that missed the gardener's face and hit him in the shoulder.

"Don Fernando! Why are you hitting me?" The voice sounded wounded, but it couldn't be from the force of the blow.

"Piss off!"

Pacheco struggled with the lock of the Mercedes while kicking wildly at the air to keep the gardener at a distance.

"But... Don Fernando... I've been waiting for you. For so, so long."

"I didn't ask you to. Leave me alone."

Another punch to push him away. Pacheco finally managed to get the car door open.

"Go on, piss off! Get lost, you crazy fuck!"

Maybe it was the punch, or the insults, or maybe it was the lack of respect. With his free hand, the gardener pulled Pacheco from the car.

"I'm not crazy, Don Fernando."

He picked up the shovel and, before they realised what was happening, landed two brutal blows to the head of the developer, who slumped to the ground. The gardener stood with one foot planted on Pacheco's chest and lifted the shovel into the air, aiming for the neck of the fallen body, ready to decapitate it. A shout stopped him: she could never remember whether it came from her or from him.

The man swung round to look at them, frozen, a second statue.

50

A dead body, a murderer, the two of them and a shovel.

They needed Matías. Without his permission, they couldn't do it; in a way, the cemetery was his.

The three of them had hauled the body into the Mercedes. Then the two men had transported him to the cemetery while she ran to find Matías.

Despite having just been woken up, the old man quickly understood what she was asking. He made only one stipulation: "Not next to my wife." He got dressed and went with her to where the others were waiting.

The gardener seemed surprisingly cool and collected given that a few minutes ago he'd killed a man – not just any man, his idol – and that the lifeless body was lying face down on the ground a couple of metres away. His initial panic at seeing the two of them pop out from behind the stone letters had given way to an almost professional calm, as if instead of burying the body of Fernando Pacheco he was about to plant a tree.

Yes, he thought, they must look more like a couple of workmen than a murderer and... and what? His accomplice? Because this had been his idea after all.

After the shout, the gardener had moved away from the body and dropped the shovel. Then he'd collapsed onto the ground. His stammering and crying showed that he was more afraid of the consequences of his actions than filled with remorse, that he was suddenly aware of the world and the life he'd just lost and was weeping for them. He'd had to grab the gardener by the shoulders then and, in a firm, persuasive voice, had planted the idea of making the body disappear.

Yes, it had been his idea, and now, seeing him leaning against the Mercedes as if it were the most natural thing in the world, he wondered if this wasn't the first time the gardener had been in a similar situation.

So he was an accomplice then.

As was she.

And as was Matías, who, after listening and making her repeat the whole story as they made their way through the streets and across the wasteland, greeted the two men with the caveat, "Not next to my wife, and I'm not doing the digging."

There was no need. The gardener said he would do it.

Matías showed him where; he wanted the three dead bodies parallel to each other and at equal intervals. Then he sat down at the foot of his wife's grave. The two of them stood leaning against the car while the gardener dug.

The ground was hard, but not once did he let them take over. They were silent, mesmerised by the rhythm of his shovelling.

When he'd finished, he rolled the body into the grave and covered it with earth, which he flattened with a few gentle pats of the shovel, the way you might pat a horse's back to calm it.

"Could you plant a shrub on top of it too?" Matías asked.

"I'll do it tomorrow."

"Don't tell a soul," he said to the gardener as they parted ways. "Not even your wife."

"I won't."

The gardener walked away with the shovel over his shoulder. They waited for him to dissolve into the darkness before the three of them got in the Mercedes.

They drove the car into the uninhabited zone, taking advantage of the huge hole in the fence made by the thwarted arsonists. Then they left it in the underground car park of the cultural centre. The three guys with the dog were no longer there. Before leaving the car, they cleaned it thoroughly to wipe off all their prints.

The day she'd met them, she'd looked for any sign that might give her a clue about their former lives, and she was disconcerted now, watching the way he conscientiously checked every last surface where any of them might possibly have laid a finger.

"Now what?" asked Matías.

51

"Now what?" Matías had asked.

He didn't have an answer.

She did: "Now we have to get out of here."

Because the people who were making it possible for Pacheco to remain in the country would end up raising the alarm. And the secret would become news.

Or because the gardener, stripped of his faith and having murdered his own deity, would end up breaking down and confessing his crime. The body was in a good place and in good company, but the gardener's conscience was not. She could imagine him pointing out the third planted shrub to police officers. Maybe he'd crumble as soon as he went back to plant that shrub.

The gardener's confession would come gushing out; he would be incapable of covering for those who'd helped him. It would be a deluge that would sweep away everything in its path.

Yes. Leaving was the only option.

She had used "we". He felt that plural embracing him. And not just him.

"Matías?" she said, turning to the old man.

"I'll have to check," he replied.

52

Their belongings did not fill the boot of the Mercedes. He brought his clothes, the money, and the play kitchen. She sat the one-armed doll on the dashboard. They parked the car almost exactly where they'd taken Pacheco's body out of it a few hours earlier.

From a distance, they watched Matías at his wife's grave.

"She'll tell him to come with us."

"How do you know?" he asked.

"Because he's dying to do it."

"And Teresa isn't a selfish woman..."

"Nah, his wife is only in his head, and his head is telling him that he wants to go with us."

Dawn was breaking.

Matías came over to them. "Can you stop at the petrol station on the way? I want to say goodbye to the Dominican," he said, climbing into the back seat.

She sat behind the wheel.

Before he got into the car, he took the blue-marked stone out of his trouser pocket and lobbed it as far as he could into the wasteland. A dull thud like a billiard ball signalled that it had rejoined its companions.

Now they could leave.

Foundry Editions
40 Randolph Street
London NW1 0SR
United Kingdom

Copyright © Rosa Ribas 2022. The author is represented by The Ella Sher Literary Agency.

First published in 2022 as *Lejos* by Tusquets Editores S.A., Barcelona
Translation © Charlotte Coombe 2024

This first edition published by Foundry Editions in 2024

The moral right of Rosa Ribas to be identified as the Author of this work has been asserted in accordance with the Copyright, Designs and Patents Act 1988.

A CIP record for this title is available from the British Library.

ISBN 978-1-7384463-4-6

Series cover design by Murmurs Design
Designed and typeset in LfA Aluminia by Tetragon, London
Printed and bound by TJ Books Limited, Padstow, Cornwall

All rights reserved. No part of this publication may be reproduced, stored in a retrieval system or transmitted in any form or by any means, electronic, mechanical, photocopying, recording or otherwise, without prior permission in writing from Foundry Editions.

foundryeditions.co.uk

CONSTANTIA SOTERIOU

Brandy Sour

Translation by Lina Protopapa

CYPRUS

When it was built in the 1950s, nothing symbolised Cyprus entering the modern world like the Ledra Palace Hotel. In Constantia Soteriou's jewel of a novel, the ambitions and shortcomings of the island's turbulent twentieth century are played out by its occupants. Among them we meet the king in exile who needs to drown his sorrows with a drink disguised to look like tea; the porter who, amidst the English roses of the hotel's gardens, secretly plants a rose from his village to make his rosebud infusions with; the UN officer who drinks lemonade to deal with the heat and the lies; and the cleaning lady who always carries her holy water with her. They are reluctant actors in history, evocatively captured in this moving, personal, and highly original portrait of civil strife and division.

Brandy Sour won the 2023 National Book Prize in Cyprus and Constantia Soteriou won the 2019 Commonwealth Short Story Prize.

MARIA GRAZIA CALANDRONE
Your Little Matter
Translation by Antonella Lettieri
ITALY

Rome, 1965. A man and a woman, excluded from Italian society, abandon their eight-month-old daughter in the Villa Borghese and take extreme action. In 2021, that child, author Maria Grazia Calandrone, sets out to discover the truth about what happened, examining the places where her mother lived, suffered, worked, and loved.

Your Little Matter is a reconstruction of the life and death of a parent, a shocking insight into the real lives of marginalised women from the Italian South, and the examination of a cause célèbre that was a catalyst for social change in Italy. Combining poetic insight with journalistic investigation, the personal and the public, the book tells a devastating story of how the institutionalised callousness of state and society can lead to tragedy.

Your Little Matter was shortlisted for the 2023 Premio Strega.

ABDELAZIZ BARAKA SAKIN
Samahani
Translation by Mayada Ibrahim and Adil Babikir
SUDAN

Samahani means "forgive me" in Swahili, but in the Arab-controlled Zanzibar of slavery, cruelty and vengeance, does forgiveness ever stand a chance? Prize-winning Sudanese author Abdelaziz Baraka Sakin follows the epic story of a spoilt Omani princess and her eunuch slave and lover, Sondus. She longs to be free from her despotic sultan father and philandering husband whilst he wants to escape his enslavement and return to the African mainland to retrieve his mutilated manhood.

With punching irony and cinematic drive, this provocative saga of the Indian Ocean slave trade explores race, class, freedom, history, and sexuality, and with a surprising humour brings English-speaking readers a compelling new take on these urgent contemporary issues.

FOUNDRY EDITIONS

1   CONSTANTIA SOTERIOU (CYPRUS)
Brandy Sour
tr. from Greek by Lina Protopapa

2   MARIA GRAZIA CALANDRONE (ITALY)
Your Little Matter
tr. from Italian by Antonella Lettieri

3   ROSA RIBAS (SPAIN)
Far
tr. from Spanish by Charlotte Coombe

4   ABDELAZIZ BARAKA SAKIN (SUDAN)
Samahani
tr. from Arabic by Mayada Ibrahim and Adil Babikir

5   ANNA PAZOS (SPAIN)
Killing the Nerve
tr. from Catalan by Laura McGloughlin and Charlotte Coombe

6   KARIM KATTAN (PALESTINE)
The Palace on Two Hills
tr. from French by Jeffrey Zuckerman

7   ESTHER GARCÍA LLOVET (SPAIN)
Spanish Beauty
tr. from Spanish by Richard Village